THE GROOM SAID MAYBE!

THE GROOM SAID MAYBE!

BY

SANDRA MARTON

MILLS & BOON®

*First published in Great Britain 1998
Large Print edition 1998
Harlequin Mills & Boon Limited,
Eton House, 18-24 Paradise Road,
Richmond, Surrey TW9 1SR*

© Sandra Myles 1998

ISBN 0 263 15678 8

*Set in Times Roman
16-9809-55734 C16-16½*

*Printed and bound in Great Britain
by Antony Rowe Ltd, Chippenham, Wiltshire*

CHAPTER ONE

DAVID CHAMBERS sat in the back row of the little
Connecticut church and did his best to appear interested in the farce taking place at the altar.

He had the sneaking suspicion he wasn't man-
aging to pull it off very well, but then, how could
he?

Lord, what utter nonsense!

The glowing bride, the nervous groom. The
profusion of flowers that made the chapel look
like a funeral parlor, the schmaltzy music, the
minister with the faultless vocal cords intoning all
the trite old platitudes about loving and honoring
and cherishing one another...

David frowned and folded his arms. He felt as
if he were sitting through the second act of a pre-
dictable comedy, with act three—The Divorce—
lurking in the wings.

"Dawn and Nicholas," the minister said, his
voice ringing out with emotion, "today you em-
bark upon the greatest adventure of your young
lives..."

5

Beside David, a woman with a helmet of dark hair sat clutching her husband's arm with one hand and a frilly handkerchief with the other. She was weeping silently and wearing a look that said she was having the time of her life. David's blue eyes narrowed. Other women were sobbing, too, even the bride's mother, who certainly should have known better than to be moved by such saccharine sentiment.

Any human being over the age of thirty should have known better, dammit, especially the ones who'd been divorced, and their number was legion. David suspected that if a voice suddenly boomed down from the choir loft and demanded that all those who'd lost the marriage wars stand up, the shuffling of feet would drown out the cherub-faced man at the altar.

''Nicholas,'' the minister said, ''will you take Dawn to be your lawful wife?''

The woman next to David gave a choked sob. David looked at her. Tears were streaming down her cheeks but her mascara was intact. Amazing, how women came prepared for these things. The makeup that didn't run, the lace hankies…you never saw a woman carrying a hankie except at weddings and funerals.

''In sickness and in health, for richer or for poorer…''

David slouched in his seat and tuned out the drivel. How much longer until it was over? He felt as if he'd spent the last week airborne, flying from D.C. to Laramie, from Laramie to London, from London to D.C. again, and then to Hartford. His eyes felt gritty, his long legs felt as if they'd been cut off at the knees thanks to the hour and a half he'd had to spend jammed into the commuter plane that had brought him to Connecticut, and sitting in this narrow wooden pew wasn't helping.

The church dated back to 1720, some white-haired old lady who might have stepped out of a Norman Rockwell painting had confided as he'd made his way inside.

David, suspecting that two and a half centuries of history would boil down to pews so closely packed that he'd end up feeling exactly the way he felt now, had offered what he'd hoped was a polite smile.

''Really,'' he'd said.

The smile hadn't worked. He knew, because the old lady had drawn back, given him a second, narrow-eyed stare that had swept over him from head to toe, taking in his height, his ponytail, his stirrup-heeled, silver-tooled boots, and then she'd raised her eyes to his and said, ''Yes, really,'' in a tone that had made it clear what she thought of a Westerner invading this pristine corner of New England.

Hell.

Maybe she was right. Maybe he shouldn't have come to the wedding. He was too tired, too cynical, too old to pretend that he was witnessing a miracle of love when the truth was that those two kids up there had about as much chance of succeeding at the thing called wedlock as a penguin had of flying to the moon.

The bride lifted worshiping eyes to her young man. Her smile trembled, full of promises. Pledges. Vows…

And right about then, David suddenly thought of the world's three biggest lies.

Every man knew them.

The check is in the mail.

Of course, I'll respect you in the morning.

Trust me.

Lie number one, at least, was gender neutral. As an attorney with offices in the nation's capitol, David had spent more time than he liked to remember sitting across his desk from clients of both sexes, either of whom had no trouble looking you straight in the eye and swearing, on a stack of Bibles, that whatever sums were in dispute were only a postal delivery away. And they usually were—so long as you assumed United States mail was routed via Mars.

The second lie was unabashedly, if embarrassingly, male. If pressed, David would have had to admit offering it himself, back in the days of his callow, hormone-crazed youth.

The memory made him smile. He hadn't thought of Martha Jean Steenburger in years, but he could picture her now, just as clearly as if it had happened yesterday.

Martha Jean, home for the summer after her freshman year at college, somehow much, much older than her eighteen years and as gloriously endowed as any sixteen-year-old boy stumbling into manhood could imagine. Martha Jean, eyeing him with interest, making him blush as she took in the height and muscle he'd added since she'd last seen him. She'd flashed him a hundred-watt smile across the barbecue pit at the Steenburgers' July Fourth party and David had gulped hard, then followed her swaying, denim-clad backside to the calf barn and up into the hayloft, where he'd nervously tried to plant a kiss on her parted lips.

"But will you respect me in the morning?" Martha Jean had said with a straight face, and when he'd managed to stutter out that of course he would, she'd chortled in a way that had made him feel dumb as well as horny and then she'd tumbled him back into the hay and introduced him to paradise.

Ah, but the third lie… The dark scowl crept over David's face again. It, too, was supposed to be strictly male, but any man over the age of puberty knew that women told it just as often and with devastating effect, because when a woman said, ''Trust me,'' it had nothing to do with sex and everything to do with love. That was what made it the most damnable falsehood. For all he knew, it had started as a whisper made by a ravishing Eve to a defenseless Adam, or a promise breathed in the ear of Samson by Delilah. It might even have been the last vow made by Guinevere to Arthur.

Trust me.

How many males had done just that, over the centuries? Millions, probably—including David.

''Well, they probably mean it, when they say it,'' a fraternity brother had once told him. ''Something about the female of the species, you know what I mean?''

It was as good an explanation as any, David figured. And all it took was one trip through the marriage mill for a man to learn that when a woman said a man could trust her, what it *really* meant was that he'd be a fool if he did. It was a hard lesson to learn, but he'd learned it.

Damn right, he had.

Put in the most basic terms, marriage was a joke.

Not that he'd given up on women. Taken at face value, he liked them still. What man wouldn't? There was nothing as pleasurable as sharing your bed and your life with a beautiful woman for a few weeks, even a few months, but when the time came to end a relationship, that was it. He wanted no tears, no regrets, no recriminations. Women didn't fault him for his attitude, either. David figured it was because he was completely up-front about his intentions, or his lack of them. He wasn't a man who made promises, not of forever-after or anything even approximating it, but he'd yet to meet a woman who'd walked away after he'd shown interest in her.

Jack Russell, one of his law partners, said it was because women saw David as an irresistible challenge. He said, too, that the day would come when David changed his mind. A wife, according to Jack, had a civilizing influence on a man. She'd run your home, plan your parties, help entertain your clients and generally get your life in hand. David agreed that that was probably true, but a good secretary and an inventive caterer could do the same things, and you didn't have to wonder what day of the week they'd turn your life upside down.

Love, if it even existed, was too dependent on men trusting women and women trusting men. It sounded good but it just didn't work...and wasn't that a hell of a thing to be brooding over right now?

David sighed, stretched his legs out as best he could, and crossed his booted ankles.

Jet lag, that was his problem, otherwise why would he be thinking such stuff? The kids standing at the altar today deserved the benefit of the doubt. Not even he was jaundiced enough to be convinced this bride would do a Jekyll and Hyde after the honeymoon ended. The girl was the daughter of an old friend. David had watched her develop from a cute kid with braces on her teeth to charming young womanhood...and he'd watched her father and mother end up in divorce court. In fact, he'd represented Chase in the divorce.

There was just no getting away from it. Marriage was an unnatural state, devised by the female of the species to suit her own purposes, and—

Bang!

What was that?

David sat up straight and swung around. The church doors had flown open; the breeze had caught them and slammed them against the walls.

A woman stood silhouetted in the late afternoon sun. A buzz of speculation swept up and down the aisles.

"Who's that?" the weeper beside him hissed to her husband. "Why doesn't she sit down? Why doesn't someone shut those doors?"

Why, indeed? David sighed, got to his feet and made his way to the rear of the church. This was going to be his day for charitable works. Annie had kissed him hello and whispered that she'd seated him with a special friend of hers.

"She's no one for you to fool around with, David," she'd said with a teasing smile. "Her name is Stephanie Willingham, and she's a widow. Be nice to her, okay?"

Well, why not? He'd been hard on the old lady outside the church but he'd make up for it by being nice to this one. He'd chat politely with the widow Willingham, maybe even waltz her once around the room, and then he'd cut out, maybe give Jessica or Helena a call before he flew back to D.C. On the other hand, he might just head home early. He had some briefs to read before tomorrow.

The woman who'd caused the commotion nodded her thanks. She was the bride's aunt; he'd met her a couple of times. She was a model, and probably accustomed to making theatrical entrances. He gave her a polite nod as she made her way past him.

David shut the doors, turned—and found himself looking straight at the most beautiful woman he'd ever seen.

She was seated in the last pew, as he had been, but on the opposite side—the groom's side—of the church. Her face was triangular, almost catlike in its delicacy; her cheekbones were high and pronounced. Her eyes were brown, her nose was straight and classic and her mouth was a soft, coral bow that hinted at endless pleasures. Her hair was the color of dark chocolate and she wore it drawn back from her face in an unadorned knot.

With heart-stopping swiftness, David found himself wondering what it would be like to take out the pins that held those silken strands and let her hair tumble into his hands.

The image was simple, but it sent a jolt of desire sizzling through his blood. He felt himself turn hard as stone.

Damn, he thought in surprise, and at that instant, the woman's eyes met his.

Her gaze was sharp and cold. It seemed to assess him, slice through the veneer afforded him by his custom-made suit and dissect his thoughts.

Hell, he thought, could she tell what had happened to him? It wasn't possible. His anatomy was behaving as if it had a will of its own, but there was no way for her to know…

But she did. She knew. He was sure of it, even though her eyes never left his. Nothing else could explain the flush that rose in her face, or the contemptuous expression that swept over it just before she turned away.

For what seemed an eternity, David remained frozen. He couldn't believe he'd had such a stupid reaction to the sight of a stranger, couldn't recall a woman looking at him with such disdain.

Primal desire gave way to equally primal rage.

He saw himself walking to where she sat, sliding into the empty seat beside her and telling her that he wouldn't have her on a bet—or better still, he could tell her that she was right, just looking at her had made him want to take her to bed, and what did she intend to do about it?

But the rules of a civilized society prevailed.

He drew a deep breath, made his way to his seat, sat down and fixed his attention on whatever in hell was happening at the altar because he was, after all, a civilized man.

Damn right, he was.

By the time the recessional echoed through the church and the bride and groom made their way out the door, he had had forgotten all about the woman...

Sure he had.

Stephanie Willingham stood at the marble-topped vanity table in the country club ladies' room and stared at her reflection in the mirror.

She didn't *look* like a woman who'd just made a damn fool of herself. That, at least, was something to be grateful for.

She took a deep breath, then let it out.

How much longer until she could make a polite exit?

Long enough, she thought, answering her own question. You couldn't sit through a wedding ceremony, hide in the powder room during the cocktail hour, then bolt before the reception without raising a few eyebrows. And that was the last thing she wanted to do because raised eyebrows meant questions, and questions required answers, and she had none.

Absolutely none.

The way that man, the one in the church, had looked at her had been bad enough. Those cool blue eyes of his, stripping her naked....

Stephanie's chin lifted. Despicable, was the only word for it.

But her reaction had been worse. Her realization that he was looking at her, that she knew exactly what was going on inside his head…that was one thing, but there was no way to explain or excuse what had happened when a rush of heat had raged through her blood.

Color flooded her cheeks at the memory.

''What is the matter with you, Stephanie?'' she said to her mirrored image.

The man had been good-looking. Handsome, she supposed, in a hard sort of way—if you liked the type. Expensively put together, but almost aggressively masculine. The hair, drawn back in a ponytail. The leanly muscled body, so well-defined within the Western-cut suit. The boots. Boots, for goodness' sake.

Clint Eastwood riding through Connecticut, she'd thought, and she should have laughed, but she hadn't. Instead, she'd felt as if someone had lit a flame deep inside her, a flame that had threatened to consume her with its heat, and that was just plain nonsense.

She didn't like men, didn't want anything to do with them ever again. Why on earth she should have reacted to the man was beyond her, especially when the look on his face had made clear what he was thinking.

Exhaustion, that had to be the answer. Flying in from Atlanta late last night, getting up so early this morning—and she'd had a bad week to begin with. First the run-in with Clare, then the meeting with Judge Parker, and finally the disappointing consultation with her own attorney. And all the while, doing what she could not to show her panic because that would only spur Clare on.

Stephanie sighed. She should never have let Annie talk her into coming to this wedding. Weddings weren't her thing to begin with. She had no illusions about them, she never had, not even before she'd married Avery, though heaven knew she wished only the best for Dawn and Nicholas. She'd certainly tried to get out of coming north, to attend this affair. As soon as the invitation had arrived, she'd phoned Annie, expressed her delight for the engaged couple, followed by her regrets, but Annie had cut her short.

"Don't give me any of that Southern cornpone," Annie had said firmly, and then her voice had softened. "You have to come to the wedding, Steffie," she'd said. "After all, you introduced Dawn and Nicholas. The kids and I will be heartbroken if you don't attend."

Stephanie smiled, put her hands to her hair and smoothed back a couple of errant strands. It had been a generous thing to say, even if it was an overstatement. She hadn't really introduced the bride and groom, she'd just happened to be driving through Connecticut on her way home after a week on Cape Cod—a week when she'd walked the lonely, out-of-season beach and tried to sort out her life. A drenching rain was falling as she'd crossed the state line from Massachusetts to Connecticut and, in the middle of it, she'd gotten a flat. She'd been standing on the side of the road, miserable and wet and cold, staring glumly at the tire, when Dawn pulled over to offer assistance. Nick had come by next. He'd shooed Dawn away from the tire and knelt down in the mud to do the job, but his eyes had been all for Dawn. As luck would have it, Annie had driven by just as Nick finished. She'd stopped, they'd all ended up introducing themselves and laughing in the downpour, and Annie had invited everyone for an impromptu cup of hot cocoa.

Stephanie's smile faded. Avery would never have understood that a friendship could be forged out of such a tenuous series of coincidences, but then, he'd never understood anything about her, not from the day they'd married until the day he'd died....

"Mrs. Willingham?"

Stephanie blinked and stared into the mirror. Dawn Cooper—the former Dawn Cooper—radiant in her white lace and satin gown, smiled at her from the doorway.

"Dawn." Stephanie swung toward the girl and embraced her. "Congratulations, darlin'. Or is it good luck?" She smiled. "I never can remember."

"It's luck, I think." The door swung shut as Dawn moved toward the mirror. "I hope it is, anyway, because I think I'm going to need it."

"You've already got all the luck you'll need," Stephanie said. "That handsome young man of yours looks as if he— Dawn? Are you all right?"

Dawn nodded. "Fine," she said brightly. "It's just, I don't know...it's just, I've been waiting and waiting for this day and now it's here, and—and—" She took a deep breath. "Mrs. Willingham?"

"Stephanie, please. Otherwise, you'll make me feel even older than I already am."

"Stephanie. I know I shouldn't ask, but—but... Did you feel, well, a little bit nervous on your wedding day?"

Stephanie stared at the girl. "Nervous?"

"Yes. You know. Sort of edgy."

"Nervous," Stephanie repeated, fixing a smile to her lips. "Well, I don't—I can't recall..."

"Not scared. I don't mean it that way. I just mean... Worried."

"Worried," Stephanie said, working hard to maintain the smile.

"Uh-huh." Dawn licked her lips. "That you might not always be as happy as you were that day, you know?"

Stephanie leaned back against the vanity table. "Well," she said, "well..."

"Oh, wow!" Dawn's eyes widened. "Oh, Mrs....oh, Stephanie. Gosh, I'm so sorry. That was such a dumb thing to ask you."

"No. Not at all. I'm just trying to think of..." *Of what lie will sound best.* "Of what to tell you."

She hadn't been nervous the day she'd married Avery, or even scared. Terrified was more accurate, terrified and desperate and almost frantic with fear...but, of course, she could never tell that to this innocent child, never tell it to anyone, and the fact she was even thinking about the possibility only proved how frazzled her nerves really were.

Stephanie smiled brightly. "Because, you understand, it was such a long time ago. Seven years, you know? Seven—"

Dawn grasped Stephanie's hands. "Forgive me, please. I'm so wrapped up in myself today that I forgot that Mr. Willingham's—that he's—that you're a widow. I didn't mean to remind you of your loss."

"No. No, really, that's all right. I'm not—"

"I am such an idiot! Talking without thinking, I mean. It's my absolutely worst trait. Even Nicky says so. Sometimes, I just babble something before I've thought it through and I get myself, *everybody,* in all kinds of trouble! Oh, I am *so* sorry, Stephanie! Can you forgive me?"

"There's nothing to forgive," Stephanie said gently, smiling at the girl.

"Are you sure?"

"Absolutely."

"No wonder you looked so sad when I came into the room. It must be so awful, losing the man you love."

Stephanie hesitated. "I suppose it is," she said after a minute.

"I can just imagine. Why, if anything ever happened to Nicky...if anything were to separate us..." Dawn's eyes grew suspiciously bright. She laughed, swung toward the mirror, yanked a tissue from the container on top of the vanity table and dabbed at her lashes. "Just listen to me! I am turning into the most maudlin creature in the whole wide world!''

''It's understandable,'' Stephanie said. ''Today's a very special one for you.''

''Yes.'' Dawn blew her nose. ''I feel like I'm on a roller coaster. Up one minute, down the next.'' She smiled. ''Thanks, Stephanie.''

''For what?''

''For putting up with me. I suppose all brides are basket cases on their wedding days.''

''Indeed,'' Stephanie said with another bright, artificial smile. ''Well, if you're sure you're okay...''

''I'm fine.''

''Would you like me to look for your mother and send her in?''

''No, don't do that. Mom's got enough to deal with today. You go on and have fun. Did you pick up your table card yet?''

Stephanie paused at the door and shook her head. ''No. No, I didn't.''

''Ah.'' Dawn grinned. ''Well, if I remember right, Mom and I put you at a terrific table.''

''Did you?'' Stephanie said with what she hoped sounded like interest.

''Uh-huh. You're sitting with a couple from New York, old friends of Mom's and Dad's. You know, from when they were still married.''

"That sounds nice."

"And my cousin and her husband. Nice guys, both of them. He's an engineer, she's a teacher."

"Well," Stephanie said, still smiling, "they all sound—"

"And with my uncle David. Well, he's not really my uncle. I mean, he's Mr. Chambers, but I've known him forever. He's a friend of my parents'. He's this really cool guy. Really cool. And handsome." Dawn giggled. "He's a bachelor, and very sexy for an older man, you know?"

"Yes. Well, he sounds—"

The door swung open and two of Dawn's bridesmaids sailed into the room on a strain of music and a gust of laughter. Stephanie saw her opportunity and took it. She blew a kiss at Dawn, smoothed down the skirt of her suit, and stepped into the corridor.

Her smile faded.

Terrific. Annie had put her at a table with an eligible bachelor. Stephanie sighed. She should have expected as much. Even though her own marriage had failed, Annie had all the signs of being an inveterate matchmaker.

"Oh," she'd said softly when she'd learned Stephanie was widowed, "that's so sad."

Stephanie hadn't tried to correct her. They didn't know each other well enough for that. The truth was, she didn't know *anyone* well enough for that. Not that anyone back home thought of her as a grieving widow. The good people of Willingham Corners had long-ago decided what she was and Avery's death hadn't changed that. At least, nobody tried to introduce her to eligible men...but that seemed to be Annie's plan today.

Stephanie gave a mental sigh as she made her way to the table where the seating cards were laid out. She could survive an afternoon with Dawn's Uncle David. He'd surely be harmless enough. Annie was clever. She'd never met Avery but she knew he'd been in his late fifties, so she'd matched Stephanie with an older man. A sexy older man, Stephanie thought with a little smile, meaning he was fifty- or sixty-something but he still had his own teeth.

She peered at the little white vellum cards, found hers and picked it up. Table seven. Well, that was something, she thought as she stepped into the ballroom. The table would be far enough from the bandstand so the music wouldn't fry her eardrums.

Stephanie wove her way between the tables, checking numbers as she went. Four, five... Yes, table seven would definitely be away from the bandstand out of deference to Uncle David, who'd probably think that the dance of the minute was the merengue. Not that it mattered. She hadn't danced in years, and she didn't miss it. She just hoped Uncle David wouldn't take it personally when she turned out to be a dud as a table partner.

Table seven. There it was, tucked almost into a corner. Most of its occupants were already seated. The trendy-looking twosome had to be the New Yorkers; the plump, sweet-faced woman with the tall, bespectacled man were sure to be the teacher and the engineer. Only Uncle David was missing, but he was certain to turn up at any second.

The little group at table seven looked up as she dropped her place card beside her plate.

"Hi," the plump woman said—and then her gaze skittered past Stephanie's shoulder, her eyes rounded and she smiled the way a woman does when she's just seen something wonderful. "And hi to you, too," she purred.

"What a small world."

Stephanie froze. The voice came from just behind her. It was male, low, and touched with satirical amusement.

She turned slowly. He was standing inches from her, the man who'd sent her pulse racing. He was every bit as tall as he'd seemed at a distance, six-one, six-two, easily. His face was a series of hard angles; his eyes were so blue they seemed to be pieces of sky. Clint Eastwood, indeed, she thought wildly, and she almost laughed.

But laughing wouldn't help. Not now. Not after her gaze fell on the white vellum card he dropped on the table beside her.

Stephanie looked up.

''Uncle David?'' she said in a choked whisper.

She remembered the way he'd looked at her the first time they'd seen each other. The smoldering glance, the lazy insolence of his smile... There was nothing of that about his expression now. His eyes were steely; the set of his mouth gave his face a harsh cast.

''And the widow Willingham.'' A thin smile curved across his mouth as he drew Stephanie's chair out from the table. ''It's going to be one hell of a charming afternoon.''

CHAPTER TWO

STEPHANIE sat down.

What else could she do? Everyone at the table was watching them, eyes bright with curiosity.

David Chambers sat down beside her. His leg brushed hers as he tucked his feet under the table. Surreptitiously, she moved her chair as far from his as she could.

He leaned toward her. "I carry no communicable diseases, Mrs. Willingham," he said dryly. "And I don't bite unless provoked."

She felt her face turn hot. His voice had been low-pitched; no one else could have heard what he'd said, but they'd wanted to—she could see it in the way they leaned forward over the table.

Say something, Stephanie told herself. Anything.

She couldn't. Her tongue felt as if it were stuck to the roof of her mouth. She cleared her throat, moistened her lips…and, mercifully, an electronic squeal from the bandstand microphone overrode all conversation in the ballroom.

The guests at table seven laughed a bit nervously.

"Those guys could use a good sound engineer," the man with the glasses said. He grinned, rose and extended his hand toward David. "Too bad that's not my speciality. Hi, nice to meet you guys. I'm Jeff Blum. And this is my wife, Roberta."

"Call me Bobbi," the plump brunette chirped, batting her lashes at David.

The other couple introduced themselves next. They looked as if they'd both been hewn out of New England granite, and had the sort of names David always irreverently thought of as Puritan holdovers.

"Hayden Crowder," the man said, extending a dry, cool hand.

"And I'm Honoria," his wife said, smiling. "And you folks are?"

"David Chambers," David said when Stephanie remained silent. He looked at her, and the grim set of his mouth softened. Okay. Maybe he was overreacting to what had happened when he'd first seen her, and to her reaction to it.

Actually, when you came down to it, *nothing* had happened—nothing that was her fault, or his. A man looked at a woman, sometimes the moment or the chemistry was just right, and that was that—although now that he was seated next to the widow Willingham, he thought wryly, he couldn't for the life of him imagine why his hormones had gone crazy back in that church. She was a looker, but so were half a dozen other women in the room. It was time to stop being an ass, remember his manners and get through the next few hours with something approaching civility.

"And the lady with me," he said pleasantly, "is—"

"Stephanie   Willingham.   Mrs.   Avery Willingham," Stephanie blurted. "And I can assure all of you that I am not here with Mr. Chambers, nor would I ever choose to be."

Bobbi Blum looked at her husband. Hayden Crowder looked at his wife. All four of them looked at Stephanie, who was trying not to look at any of them.

Ohmygod!

What on earth had possessed her? It was such an incredibly stupid thing to have said, especially after the man seated beside her had made an attempt, however late and unwanted, at showing he had, at least, some semblance of good manners.

"Do tell," Bobbi Blum said with a bright smile. She sat back as the waiter set glasses of champagne before them. "Well, that's certainly very, ah, interesting."

Honoria Crowder shot a brilliant smile across the table. "Champagne," she said briskly. "Isn't that nice? I always say champagne's the only thing to serve at weddings, isn't that right, Hayden?"

Hayden Crowder swallowed hard. Stephanie could see his Adam's apple bob up and down in his long, skinny neck.

"Indeed you do, my dear."

"Oh, I agree." Jeff Blum, eager to do his part, nodded vigorously. "Don't I always say that, too, Bobbi?"

Bobbi Blum turned a perplexed smile on her husband. "Don't you always say what, dear?"

"That champagne is—that it's whatever Mrs. Crowder just said it was."

"Do call me Honoria," Honoria said.

Silence settled over the table again.

Stephanie's hands were knotted together in her lap. Everyone had said something in an attempt to ease the tension—everyone but David Chambers.

He was looking at her. She could feel the weight of his gaze. Why didn't he say something? Why didn't *she* say something? A witty remark, to take the edge off. A clever one, to turn her awful words into a joke.

When was the band going to start playing?

As if on cue, the trumpet player rose to his feet and sent a shattering tattoo of sound out into the room.

"And now," the bandleader said, "let's give a warm welcome to Dawn and Nicholas!"

The Crowders, then the Blums, looked toward the dance floor as the introductions rolled on. Stephanie breathed a small sigh of relief. Perhaps David Chambers's attention was on the newlyweds, too. Her hand closed around her small, apricot-silk purse. Carefully, she moved back her chair. Now might be the perfect time to make another strategic retreat to the ladies' room...

"Leaving so soon, Mrs. Willingham?"

Stephanie froze. Then, with as much hauteur as she could manage, she turned her head toward David Chambers. His expression was polite and courteous; she was sure he looked the picture of civility—unless you were sitting as close to him as she was, and you could see the ridicule in his eyes.

Okay. It was time to take a bite, however small, of humble pie.

"Mr. Chambers." She cleared her throat. "Mr. Chambers, I suppose—what I said before—I didn't mean..."

He smiled coolly and bent toward her, his eyes on hers.

"An apology?"

"An explanation." Stephanie sat up straight. "I was rude, and I didn't intend to be."

"Ah. What did you intend to be, then?" His smile tilted and he moved closer, near enough to make her heartbeat quicken. For one foolish instant, she'd thought he was going to kiss her.

"I simply meant to make it clear that you and I were not together."

"You certainly did that."

"I'm sure Annie meant well, when she seated us this way, but—"

"Annie?"

"Annie Cooper. Surely, you know—"

"You were seated on the groom's side."

"I know both the bride and the groom, Mr. Chambers."

"But you're Annie's guest."

"I can't see of what possible interest it could be to you, sir."

Neither could David—except that it had occurred to him, as he'd gone down the receiving line, that word had it that the groom's uncle, Damian Skouras, had a mistress in attendance at the wedding. Perhaps Stephanie Willingham was she. Or perhaps she was a former mistress. Or a future one. It was a crazy world out there; there was no telling what complications you got into when you drew up guest lists. He'd avoided the problem, his one time in the matrimonial sweepstakes. You didn't draw up a guest list when you said "I do" at city hall.

"Humor me, Mrs. Willingham," David said with a chilly smile. "Why did you choose to sit on the groom's side?"

"What do you do for a living, Mr. Chambers?"

"I don't see what that has to do with my question."

"Suppose you humor *me,* and answer it."

David's frown deepened. "I'm an attorney."

"Ah. Well, I suppose that explains it."

"Explains what?" David said, his eyes narrowing.

"Your tendency to interrogate."

"I beg your pardon, Mrs. Willingham. I did not—"

"I must admit, I find it preferable to your tendency to strip a woman naked with your eyes."

The band segued from a bouncy rendition of "My Girl" to a soft, sighing "Stardust." Stephanie's words rose clearly over the plaintive opening notes.

A strangled gasp burst from Honoria Crowder's lips. Her champagne glass tipped over and a puddle of pale golden wine spread across the white tablecloth.

"Oh, my," Honoria twittered, "how clumsy of me!"

Bobbi Blum snatched at a napkin. "Here," she said, "let me get that."

Saved by the spill, Stephanie thought hysterically. She smiled blindly at the waiter as he served their first course. The Crowders and the Blums grabbed their oyster forks and attacked their shrimp cocktails with a fervor she suspected was born of the desire to leap to their feet and run from what was turning into the kind of encounter that ends with one of the parties bleeding.

If you had any brains, Stephanie told herself, you'd do the same...

Instead, she picked up her fork and began to stuff food into her mouth because if she was chewing and swallowing, maybe—just maybe—she'd stop saying things that only made this impossible mess messier.

"I don't."

Stephanie's head snapped up. She looked at David, and the smug little smile on his face sent a chill straight into the marrow of her bones.

"Don't what?" Bobbi Blum said, and everyone leaned forward in eager anticipation.

"Don't have a tendency to strip women naked with my eyes." His smile tilted, and his gaze swept over Stephanie again, sending a flood of color to her cheeks. "Not indiscriminately, that is. I only focus that sort of attention on beautiful women who look to be in desperate need of—"

Music blared from the bandstand.

Forks clattered to the table.

The Crowders and the Blums pushed back their chairs and rushed to the dance floor.

Stephanie sat very still, though she could damn near feel the blood churning in her veins. She thought about slugging the man beside her, but that wouldn't be fair to Annie, or Dawn, or Nicholas. Besides, ladies didn't do such things. The woman—the girl—she'd once been might have. Would have. Steffie Horton would have balled up her fist and shot a right cross straight to David Chambers's square jaw.

A tremor went through her. Steffie Horton would have done exactly what Stephanie Willingham had been doing all afternoon. She'd have been rude, and impolite; she'd have spoken her mind without thinking. She might even have reacted to the heat in a stranger's eyes. It was in her genes, after all. Avery had been wrong about a lot of things, but not about that.

What was wrong with her today? She was behaving badly. And even when David Chambers had held out an olive branch—a ragged one, it was true, but an olive branch nevertheless—she'd slapped it out of his hand.

Stephanie took a deep breath and turned toward him.

"Mr. Chambers…"

Her words caught in her throat. He was smiling…no, he wasn't. Not really. His lips were drawn back from his teeth in a way that reminded her of a mastiff Avery had owned when she'd first married him and gone to live in the house on Oak Hill—when she'd still been young enough, stupid enough, to have thought their arrangement could work.

"Oh," she'd said, "just look at your dog, Avery. He's smiling at me."

And Avery had guffawed and slapped his knees and said that he'd truly picked himself a backwoods ninny if she thought that was a smile, and maybe she'd like to offer the mastiff her hand and see if it came back with all the fingers still attached.

"Yes?" David said politely. "Did you have something you wanted to say?"

"No," Stephanie said just as politely. "Not a thing."

He nodded. "That's fine. I think I've just about run out of conversation, myself—except to point out that, with any luck at all, we'll never have the misfortune to meet again.'' His wolfish smile flickered. ''Have I left anything out?''

''Not a thing. In fact, I doubt I could have put it better.''

David unfolded his napkin and placed it in his lap. Stephanie did the same.

''*Bon appétit,* Mrs. Willingham,'' David said softly.

''*Bon appétit,* Mr. Chambers,'' Stephanie replied, and she picked up her fork, speared a shrimp, and began to eat.

More toasts were drunk, the wedding cake sliced. The Blums and the Crowders continued to make themselves scarce, appearing only from time to time and then just long enough to gobble down a few mouthfuls of each course as it was served.

''We just adore dancing,'' Bobbi Blum gushed between the *Boeuf aux Champignons* and the salad.

''Same with us,'' Hayden Crowder said as his wife sat smiling uneasily beside him. ''Why, we never sit very long at these shindigs, no matter who's seated at our table, do we, honey?''

''Never,'' Honoria said, and jumped to her feet. ''We never stay seated, no matter what.''

David watched with a thin smile as both couples hurried off. Then he pushed his plate aside, tilted back his chair and folded his arms over his chest.

"Well," he said after a minute, "this is one wedding they're never going to forget."

Stephanie glanced up. "No. I suppose not."

Across the dance floor, the Blums and the Crowders were standing in a little huddle, looking back at table seven as if they expected either the police or the men with straitjackets to show up at any minute.

David couldn't help it. He laughed.

Stephanie's lips twitched. "It isn't funny," she said stiffly—and then she laughed, too.

He looked at her. Her cheeks had taken on a delicate flush and there was a glint in her dark eyes that hadn't been there before. She looked young, and beautiful, and suddenly he knew that he'd been kidding himself when he'd told himself she wasn't the most beautiful woman in this room, because she was. She was more than beautiful, she was indescribably gorgeous.

And he'd been sniping at her for the past hour. Damn, he had to be crazy! Everything he'd done had been crazy, since he'd laid eyes on her. He should have sat down beside her, introduced himself, asked her if he could see her again. He should have told her she was the most beautiful woman he'd ever met....

He could still do all of that. It wasn't too late and, heaven knew, it was the best idea he'd had in the past couple of hours.

"Mrs. Willingham. Stephanie. About what happened earlier..." Her face lifted toward his. David smiled. "In the church, I mean."

"Nothing happened," she said quickly.

"Come on, let's not play games. Something happened, all right. I looked at you, you looked at me..."

"Mr. Chambers—"

"David."

"Mr. Chambers." Stephanie folded her hands in her lap. "Look, I know this isn't your fault. I mean, I know Annie probably set this up."

"Probably?" He laughed. "Of course, she set this up. You're unattached. You *are* unattached, aren't you?"

Stephanie nodded. "I'm a widow."

"Yeah, well, I'm divorced. So Annie took a look at her guest list, saw my name, saw yours, and that was it. It's in her blood, though I can't imagine why, considering her own record."

Color flooded Stephanie's face. "I assure you, Mr. Chambers, I have absolutely no wish to marry, ever again."

"Whoa!" David held up his hands. "One step at a time, Mrs. Willingham—and before anybody takes that step, let me assure *you* that I'd sooner waltz Mrs. Blum around the dance floor for the next three weeks than ever do something as stupid as tying another knot. Not in this lifetime. Or any other, for that matter.''

Stephanie tried not to smile. ''There's nothing wrong with Mrs. Blum.''

''She dances on her husband's feet,'' David said, ''and she outweighs the both of us.'' Stephanie laughed. His smile tilted, and his gaze dropped to her mouth. ''You have a nice laugh, Stephanie.''

''Mr. Chambers...''

''David. Surely we've insulted each other enough to be on a first-name basis.''

''David, maybe we did get off on the wrong foot, but—''

''So did Mrs. Blum.''

She smiled again, and his heart lifted. She really did have a nice smile.

''Let's just forget it, shall we?''

''I'd like that, very much—especially since it was all my fault.''

''That's kind of you, David, but, well, I was to blame, too. I—I saw the way you were looking at me in the church, you know, when you went to shut the doors, and—and I thought...'' She took a deep breath. "All I'm trying to say is that I didn't mean to be so—so—"

"Impolite?" he asked innocently. "Judgmental? Is that the word you're looking for?"

Laughter glinted in her eyes.

"You're pushing your luck," she said. "Putting words in my mouth that way."

He thought of what he'd like to do with that mouth, how badly he wanted to taste it, and cleared his throat.

"Ah," he said, shaking his head sadly, "and here I thought the widow Willingham was about to offer a full apology for her behavior. So much for the mystique of Southern good manners."

"My manners are usually impeccable. And how can you be so certain I'm from the South?"

He chuckled. "'An' how can you be so suhtain Ah'm from th' South?'" he said.

Stephanie tried not to smile, but it was impossible. "I'm glad my accent amuses you, Mr. Chambers."

"I promise you, Mrs. Willingham, I'm not laughing at you. Matter of fact, I like your drawl. It's very feminine."

"If you're waiting for me to say I like the sound of your Montana twang, Mr. Chambers—"

"Montana?" David slapped his hand over his heart. "Good God, woman, you do know how to wound a man. I'm from Wyoming."

"Oh."

"Oh? Is that all you can say, after you accuse me of being from a state where the cows outnumber the people three to one?" He grinned. "At least, in Wyoming, we only have one critter that walks upright for every two point something that moos."

Stephanie laughed politely. "My apologies."

"Apologies accepted. And, just for the record, I have no accent."

Her smile was warm and open this time. He had an accent; she was sure he knew it as well as she did. His voice was low and husky; it reminded her of high mountains and wide open spaces, of a place where the night sky would be bright with stars and the grassy meadows would roll endlessly toward the horizon....

"Gotcha," he said softly.

Stephanie blinked. "What?"

"You smiled," David said with a little smile of his own. "Really smiled. And I agree."

"Agree about what?" she said in total confusion.

"That we got off to the wrong start."

She considered the possibility. Perhaps they had. He seemed a nice enough man, this friend of Annie's. There was no denying his good looks, and he had a sense of humor, too. Not that she was interested in him. Not that she'd ever be interested in any man. Still, that was no reason not to be polite. Pleasant, even. This was just one day out of her life. One afternoon. And what had he done, when you came down to it? Looked at her, that was all. Just looked at her, and even though she hated it, she was accustomed to it.

Men had always looked at her, even before Avery had come along.

Besides, she wasn't guiltless. For one heart-stopping instant, for one quick spin of the planet, she'd looked at David and felt—she'd felt...

"Stephanie?"

She raised her head. David was watching her, eyes dark and intense.

"How about we begin over?"

He held out his hand. Stephanie hesitated. Then, very slowly and carefully, she lifted her hand from her lap and placed it in his.

"That's it," he said softly. His fingers closed around hers. They were warm, and hard, and calloused. That surprised her. Despite what he'd said about being from the west, despite the cowboy boots and the ponytail and the incredible width of his shoulders, everything about him whispered of wealth and power. Men like that didn't have hands that bore the imprint of hard work, not in her world.

He bent his head toward hers. She knew she ought to pull back but she couldn't. His eyes were still locked on hers. They seemed to draw her in.

"You're a very beautiful woman, Stephanie."

"Mr. Chambers…"

"I thought we'd progressed to David."

"David." Stephanie ran the tip of her tongue over her lips. She saw him follow the motion with his eyes and the tiny flame that had come to life hours before sprang up again deep within her. A warning tingled along her skin. "David," she said again, "I think—I think it's nice that we made peace with each other, but—"

"We should be honest, too."

"I am being honest. I don't want—"

"Yes. You *do* want." His voice had taken on a roughness. A huskiness. It made the trembling flame within her burn brighter. "We both do."

"No!"

He could feel the sudden tension radiating from her fingers to his. Don't be a fool, David told himself fiercely. There was plenty of time. The longer it took to go from that first beat of sexual awareness to the bed, the greater the pleasure. He'd lived long enough to know that.

But he couldn't slow down. Not with this woman. He wanted her, now. Right now. He wanted her beneath him, her body naked to his hands and mouth, her eyes liquid with desire as he touched her, entered her.

"Come with me," he said urgently. "I have a car outside. We'll find a hotel."

"You bastard!" She tore her hand from his. "Is that what the past few minutes were all about?"

"No," he said, trying to deny it, as much to himself as to her. He felt as if he were standing on the edge of a precipice, that the slightest gust of wind could come by and send him tumbling out into space. He'd met women before, wanted them, but not like this. Not with a need so fierce it obliterated everything else. "Stephanie—"

"Don't 'Stephanie' me!" She shoved back her chair. Her face was flushed; she glared at him, her mouth trembling. "You've wasted your time, Mr. Chambers. I know your game."

"Dammit, it isn't a game! I saw you, and I wanted you. And you wanted me. That's why you're so angry, isn't it? Because you felt the same thing, only you're afraid to admit it."

"I'm not afraid of anything, Mr. Chambers, especially not of a man like you."

It was a lie. She *was* afraid; he saw it in her eyes, in the feverish color in her cheeks.

"I know your type, sir. You see a woman like me, your mind goes rolling straight into the gutter."

"What?" he said with an incredulous little laugh.

"As for what I want… You flatter yourself. I'd no more want you in my bed than I'd want a cottonmouth moccasin there! Why would I? Why would any woman in her right mind want to subjugate herself to a—a—"

"Hey, guys, how's it going?"

Stephanie clamped her lips together. She and David both looked up. Annie Cooper stood over them, smiling happily.

"Annie," David said after a minute. He cleared his throat. "Hello."

"I hated to interrupt," Annie said, smiling. "You two were so deep in conversation."

Stephanie looked at David, then at Annie. "Uh, yes. Yes, we were." She smiled brightly. "It's a lovely wedding, Annie. Really lovely."

Annie pulled out a chair and sat down. "So," she said slyly, "I figured right, hmm?"

"Figured right?"

"About you guys." Annie grinned. "Dawn and I were doing the seating chart and Dawn said to me, 'Mom, except for Nicky, the best-looking man at the wedding is going to be Uncle David.' And I said to her, 'Well, except for you, my gorgeous, too-young-to-be-a-bride daughter, the most beautiful woman at the wedding is going to be your very own cupid, Stephanie.'"

"Annie," David said, "listen—"

"So my brilliant offspring and I put our heads together and, *voilà,* we put the pair of you at the same table." Annie smiled. "Clever, if I say so myself, no?"

"No," Stephanie said. "I mean, I'm sure you thought it was, Annie, but—"

Annie laughed. "Relax, you two. We won't expect you to announce your engagement or anything. Not today, anyway... My gosh, Stef, I'm making you blush. And David...if looks could kill, I'd be lying in a heap on the floor." A furrow appeared between her eyes. "Don't tell me we goofed! Aren't you two having a good time? Haven't you hit it off?"

"We're having a terrific time," Stephanie said quickly. "Aren't we...David?"

David smiled tightly and shoved back his chair. "Better than terrific," he said. "Excuse me for a minute, will you? I'm going to get myself a drink.

Annie? Stephanie? Can I bring you ladies something?''

''Nothing for me, thank you,'' Annie said.
''I'm on overload as it is.''

A bludgeon, Stephanie thought. ''White wine,''
she said, because Annie was looking at her ex-
pectantly.

David nodded. ''Be right back.''

Damn, he thought grimly as he made his way
across the ballroom, damn! Why in hell was he
making such a fool of himself with Stephanie
Willingham? She was wild as a mustang and
beautiful as a purebred, and okay, there wasn't
another woman in the place who could hold a
candle to her, but either he'd read the signs wrong
and she wasn't interested, or she liked to play
games. Whichever it was, why should he care?
The world was filled with beautiful women and
finding ones who were interested had never been
a problem. They seemed to go for his type, whatever that was.

It was just that there was something about
Stephanie. All that frost. Or maybe the heat. It
was crazy. A woman couldn't be hot and cold at
the same time, she couldn't look at a man as if
she wanted to be in his arms one minute and
wanted to slap him silly the next unless she was

a tease, and instinct told him that whatever she was, she was not that.

What he ought to do was walk right on past the bar, out the door and to his car. Drive to the airport, catch the shuttle back to D.C....

David's brows lifted. He began to smile.

"Chase?" he called.

There was no mistaking the set of shoulders in front of him. It was his old pal, Chase Cooper, the father of the bride.

Chase turned around, saw David, and held out his hand. "David," he said, and then both men grinned and gave each other a quick bear hug. "How're you doing, man?"

"Fine, fine. How about you?"

Chase lifted his glass to his lips and knocked back half of the whiskey in it in one swallow.

"Never been better. What'll you have?"

"Scotch," David said to the bartender. "A single malt, if you have it, on the rocks. And a glass of Chardonnay."

Chase smiled. "Don't tell me that you're here with a lady. Has the love bug bitten you, too?"

"Me?" David laughed. "The wine's for a lady at my table. The love bug already bit me, remember? Once bitten, twice shy. No, not me. Never again."

"Yeah." Chase nodded, and his smile flickered. "I agree. You marry a woman, she turns into somebody else after a couple of years."

"You've got it," David said. "Marriage is a female fantasy. Promise a guy anything to nab him, then look blank when he expects you to deliver." The bartender set the Scotch in front of David, who lifted the glass to his lips and took a drink. "Far as I'm concerned, a man's got a housekeeper, a cook, and a good secretary, what more does he need?"

"Nothing," Chase said a little too quickly, "not one thing."

David glanced back across the ballroom. He could see Stephanie, sitting alone at the table. Annie had left, but she hadn't bolted. It surprised him.

"Unfortunately," he said, trying for a light touch, "there *is* one other thing a man needs, and it's the thing that most often gets guys like you and me in trouble."

"Yeah." Chase followed his gaze, then lifted his glass and clinked it against David's. "Well, you and I both know how to deal with that little problem. Bed 'em and forget 'em, I say."

David grinned. "I'll drink to that."

"To what? What are you guys up to, hidden away over here?"

Both men turned around. Dawn, radiant in white lace, and with Nick at her side, beamed at them.

"Daddy," she said, kissing her father's cheek. "And Mr. Chambers. I'm so glad you could make it."

"Hey." David smiled. "What happened to 'Uncle David'? I kind of liked the honorary title." He held out his hand to Nicholas, said all the right things, and stood by politely until the bridal couple moved off.

Chase sighed. "That's the only good thing comes of a marriage," he said. "A kid of your own, you know?"

David nodded. "I agree. I'd always hoped..." He shrugged. "Hey, Cooper," he said with a quick grin, "you stand around a bar long enough, you get maudlin. Anybody ever tell you that?"

"Yes," Chase said. "My attorney, five years ago when we got wasted after my divorce was finalized."

The men smiled at each other, and then David slapped Chase lightly on the back.

"You ought to circulate, man. There's a surprising assortment of good-looking single women here, in case you hadn't noticed."

"For a lawyer," Chase said with a chuckle, "sometimes you manage to come up with some pretty decent suggestions. So, what's with the brunette at your table? She spoken for?''

"She is," David said gruffly. "For the present, at least."

Chase grinned. "You dirty dog, you. Well, never mind. I'll case the joint, see what's available."

"Yeah." David grinned in return. "You do that."

The men made their goodbyes. Chase set off in one direction, David in the other. The dance floor had grown crowded; the band had launched into a set of sixties' standards that seemed to have brought out every couple in the room. David wove between them, his gaze fixed on Stephanie. He saw her turn and look in his direction. Their eyes met; he felt as if an electric current had run through his body.

"Whoops." A woman jostled his elbow. "Sorry."

David looked around, nodded impatiently as she apologized. The music ceased. The dancers applauded, and the crowd parted.

Table seven was just ahead. The Blums were there, and the Crowders.

But Stephanie Willingham was gone.

CHAPTER THREE

THE only thing worse than leaving Washington on a Friday was returning to it on a Monday.

Every politician and lobbyist who earned his or her living toiling in the bureaucratic fields of the District of Columbia flew home for the weekend. That was the way it seemed, anyway, and if Friday travel was a nightmare of clogged highways, jammed airports and overbooked flights, Mondays were all that and more. There was something about the start of the workweek that made for woefully short tempers.

David had made careful plans to avoid what he thought of as the Monday Morning Mess. He'd told his secretary to book him out of Hartford on a late Sunday flight and when that had turned out to be impossible, he'd considered how long it would be before he could make a polite exit from the Cooper wedding reception and instructed her to ticket him out of Boston. It was only another hour, hour and a half's drive.

A simple enough plan, he had figured.

But nothing was simple, that Sunday.

By midafternoon, hours before he'd expected to leave Stratham, David was in his rented car, flooring the pedal as he flew down the highway. He was in a mood even he knew could best be described as grim.

Now what? He had hours to kill before his flight from Boston, and he had no wish whatsoever to sit around an airport, cooling his heels.

Not ever, but especially not now. Not when he was so annoyed he could have chewed a box of nails and spit them out as staples.

There was always the flight out of Hartford, the one he'd turned down as being scheduled too early. Yes. He'd head for Bradley Airport, buy a ticket on that flight instead.

Maybe he should phone, check to see if there was an available seat.

No. What for? Bradley was a small airport. It didn't handle a lot of traffic. Why would a plane bound for D.C. on a Sunday afternoon be booked up?

David made a sharp right, skidded a little as he made up his mind, and took the ramp that led north toward the airport.

The sooner he got out of here, the better. Why hang around this part of the world any longer than necessary?

"No reason," he muttered through his teeth, "none at all."

He glanced down, saw that the speedometer was edging over sixty. Was fifty-five the speed limit in Connecticut, or was it sixty-five? Back home—back in his *real* home, Wyoming—people drove at logical speeds, meaning you took a look at the road and the traffic and then, the sky was the limit.

But not here.

"Hell," he said, and goosed the car up to sixty-five.

He'd done what had been required, even if he had left the reception early. He'd toasted the bride and groom, paid his respects to Annie, shaken Chase's hand and had a drink with him. That was enough. If other people wanted to hang around, dance to a too loud band, tuck into too rich food, make a pretense of having a good time, that was their business.

Besides, he'd pretty much overstayed his welcome at table seven. David figured the Blums and the Crowders would make small talk for a month out of what had gone on between him and Stephanie, but they'd also probably cheered his defection.

The needle on the speedometer slid past seventy.

"Leaving so soon?" Bobbi Blum had asked, after he'd made a circuit of the ballroom and then paused at the table just long enough to convince the Blums and the Crowders that he really was insane. Her voice had been sweet, her smile syrupy enough to put a diabetic into a coma, but the look in her eyes said, "Please, oh, please, don't tell us you're just stepping outside to have a smoke."

Maybe it had something to do with the way he'd demanded to know if any of them had seen Stephanie leave.

"I did," Honoria had squeaked, and it was only when he'd heard that high-pitched voice that reality had finally made its way into David's overcooked brain and he'd realized he was acting like a man one card short of a full deck.

And for what reason? David's mouth thinned, and he stepped down harder on the gas pedal.

It wasn't Honoria's fault—it wasn't anybody's fault—that he'd let Stephanie Willingham poison his disposition before she'd vanished like a rabbit inside a magician's hat.

"Give us a break, Chambers," he muttered.

Who was he trying to fool? It was somebody's fault, all right. His. He'd homed in on Stephanie like a heat-seeking missile and that wasn't his style. He was a sophisticated man with a sophisticated approach. A smile, a phone call. Flowers, chocolates…he wasn't in the habit of coming on to a woman with all the subtlety of a cement truck.

He could hardly blame her for leaving without so much as a goodbye.

Not that he cared. Well, yeah, he cared that he'd made a fool of himself, but aside from that, what did it matter? David's hands relaxed on the steering wheel; his foot eased off the pedal. The widow Willingham was something to look at, and yes, she was an enigma. He'd bet anything that the colder-than-the-Antarctic exterior hid a hotter-than-the-Tropics core.

Well, let some other poor sucker find out.

He preferred his women to be soft. Feminine. Independent, yes, but not so independent you felt each encounter was only a heartbeat away from stepping into a cage with a tiger. The bottom line was that this particular babe meant nothing to him. Two, three hours from now, he'd probably have trouble remembering what she looked like. Those dark, unfathomable eyes. That lush mouth. The silken hair, and the body that just wouldn't quit, even though she'd hidden it inside a tailored suit the color of ripe apricots.

Apricot. That was the shade, all right. Not that he'd ever consciously noticed. If somebody had said, "Okay, Chambers, what was the widow wearing?" he'd have had to shrug and admit he hadn't any idea.

Not true. He *did* have an idea. His foot bore down on the accelerator. A very specific one. His brain had registered all the pertinent facts, like the shade of the fabric. And some nonpertinent ones, like the way the jacket fit, clinging to the rise of her breasts, then nipping in at her waist before flaring out gently over her hips. Or the way the skirt had just kissed her knees. He'd noticed the color of her stockings, too. They'd been pale gray. And filmy, like the sheerest silk.

Were they stockings? Or were they panty hose? Who was it who'd invented panty hose, anyway? Not a man, that was certain. A man would have understood the importance of keeping women— beautiful, cool-to-the-eye women—in thigh-length stockings and garter belts. Maybe that was what she'd been wearing beneath that chastely tailored suit. Hosiery that would feel like cobwebs to his hands as he peeled them down her legs. A white lace garter belt, and a pair of tiny white silk panties....

The shrill howl of a siren pierced the air. David shot a glance at the speedometer, muttered a quick, sharp word and pulled onto the shoulder of the road. The flashing red lights of a police cruiser filled his rearview mirror as it pulled in behind him.

David shut off the engine and looked in his mirror again. The cop sauntering toward him was big. He was wearing dark glasses, even though the afternoon was clouding over, as if he'd seen one old Burt Reynolds' movie too many. David sighed and let down his window. Then, without a word, he handed over his driver's license.

The policeman studied the license, then David.

"Any idea how fast you were tooling along there, friend?" he asked pleasantly.

David wrapped his hands around the steering wheel and blew out a breath.

"Too fast."

"You got that right."

"Yeah."

"That's it? Just, 'yeah'? No story? No excuse?"

"None you'd want to hear," David said after a couple of seconds.

"Try me," the cop said. David looked at him, and he laughed. "What can I tell you? It's been a slow day."

A muscle clenched in David's jaw. "I just met a woman," he said. "I didn't like her. She didn't like me, and I think—I know—I pretty much made an ass of myself. It shouldn't matter. I mean, I know I'll never see her again…but I can't get her out of my head.''

There was a silence, and then the cop sighed.

"Listen," he said, "you want some advice?" He handed David his license, took off his dark glasses and put his huge hands on the window ledge. "Forget the babe, whoever she is. Women are nothing but grief and worry.''

David looked at the cop. "That they are.''

"Damn right. Hey, I should know. I been married seven years.''

"I should, too. I've been *divorced* seven years.''

The two men looked at each other. Then the cop straightened up.

"Drive slowly, pal. The life you save, and all that…''

David smiled. "I will. And thanks.''

The cop grinned. "If guys don't stick together, the babes will win the war.''

"They'll probably win it anyway," David said, and drove off.

A war.

That's was what it was, all right.

Men against women. Hell, why limit it? It was male against female. No species was safe. One sex played games, the other sex went crazy.

David strode into the departures terminal at the airport, his garment carrier slung over his shoulder.

That was what all that nonsense had been today. A war game. The interval with the policeman had given him time to rethink things, and he'd finally figured out what had happened at that wedding.

Stephanie Willingham had been on maneuvers.

It wasn't that he'd come on too hard. It was that she'd been setting up an ambush from the moment in church when they'd first laid eyes on each other. He'd made the mistake of letting his gonads do his thinking and, bam, he'd fallen right into the trap.

On the other hand… David frowned as he took his place on the tail end of a surprisingly long line at the ticket counter. On the other hand, the feminine stratagems she'd used were unlike any he'd ever experienced.

Some women went straight into action. They'd taken the equality thing to heart. "Hello," they'd purr, and then they'd ask a few questions—were you married, involved, whatever—and if you gave the right answers, they made it clear they were interested.

He liked women who did that, admired them for being straightforward, though in his heart of hearts, he had to admit he still enjoyed doing things the old-fashioned way. There was a certain pleasure in doing the pursuing. If a woman played just a little hard to get, it heightened the chase and sweetened the moment of surrender.

But Stephanie Willingham had gone overboard.

She hadn't just played hard to get. She'd played impossible.

The line shuffled forward and David shuffled along with it.

Maybe he really wasn't her type. Maybe she hadn't found his looks to her liking.

No. There was such a thing as modesty but there was such a thing as honesty, too, and the simple truth was that he hadn't had trouble getting female attention since his voice had gone down and his height had gone up, way back in junior high school.

Maybe she just didn't like men. Maybe her interests lay elsewhere. Anything was possible in today's confused, convoluted, three-and-four-gender world.

No. Uh-uh. Stephanie Willingham was all female. He'd bet everything he had on that.

What was left, then? If she hadn't found him repugnant, if she wasn't interested in women…

David frowned. Maybe she was still in love with her husband.

"Hell," he said, under his breath. The elderly woman standing in front of him looked around, eyebrows lifted. David blushed. "Sorry. I, uh, I didn't expect this line to be so long…"

"Never expect anything," the woman said. "My Earl always said that. If you don't expect anything, you can't be disappointed."

Philosophy, on a ticket line in Connecticut? David almost smiled. On the other hand, it was probably good advice. And he'd have taken it to heart, if he'd needed to. But he didn't, because he was never going to see Stephanie Willingham again. How come he kept forgetting that?

End of problem. End of story. The line staggered forward. By the time David reached the ticket counter, he was smiling.

"Mrs. Willingham?"

Honoria Crowder let the door to the ladies' room of the Stratham Country Club swing shut behind her.

"Mrs. Willingham? Stephanie?"

Honoria peered at the line of closed stalls. Then she rolled her eyes, bent down and checked for feet showing under the doors. A pair of shiny black pumps peeped from beneath the last door on the end.

"He's gone," she said.

The door swung open and Stephanie looked out. "You're sure?"

"Positive. The coast is clear. Mr. Chambers left."

"You saw him go?"

"With my very own eyes, Stephanie. He gave us the third degree and when we'd convinced him you'd left, he did, too."

"I'm terribly sorry to have put you through all this, Mrs. Crowder."

"Honoria."

"Honoria." Stephanie hesitated. "I know my behavior must seem—it must seem..." Odd? Bizarre? Strange? "Unusual," she said. "And I'm afraid I really can't explain it."

"No need," Honoria said politely.

It was a lie. Honoria Crowder would have sold her soul for an explanation. She'd felt like a voyeur, watching the sparks bounce between the Chambers man and this woman. She'd said as much to Hayden, even added that anybody standing too close could almost have gotten singed. Hayden had given one of his prissy little smiles as if he had no idea what she was talking about—but Bobbi Blum, who'd turned out to be lots more perceptive than she'd looked, had leaned over as she'd danced by in her husband's arms and whispered that what Honoria had just said was God's honest truth.

"I'm not sure if those two are going to haul off and slug each other senseless, or if they're going to grab hold of each other and just..." She'd blushed. "Just, you know..."

Honoria knew. She wouldn't have put it quite so bluntly, but yes, that about summed things up. The Willingham woman and that man had turned out to be the entertainment of the day.

"It isn't as if I was afraid of him, you understand."

Honoria blinked. "Beg pardon?"

"That man. David Chambers." Stephanie cleared her throat. "I, uh, I wouldn't want anyone to think he'd, you know, threatened me or anything."

"Oh. Well, no, no, actually I didn't—"

"It's just that he...that I...that I felt it was best if...if..."

If what, Stephanie? Why are you acting like such an idiot? Why are you hiding in the ladies' room, as if this were prom night and you'd just discovered that your slip was showing?

Stephanie grabbed for the doorknob. "Thanks again."

The door swung shut, and that was it. Honoria Crowder sighed, washed her hands, and headed back to table seven.

"Fascinating," Bobbi Blum said when Honoria told her the latest details over decaf and wedding cake.

"Interesting," Honoria corrected.

Bobbi leaned closer. "Wasn't he just drop-dead gorgeous?"

Honoria opened her mouth and started to correct her there, as well. Drop-dead gorgeous was such a New York kind of phrase. It was overblown. Overdone. Over-dramatic...

But my goodness, it was accurate.

That build. Those eyes. The hair. The face... Honoria's inborn New England sense of reticence deserted her, and she sighed.

"Drop-dead gorgeous, indeed," she murmured.

David Chambers surely was.

The wonder of it was that Stephanie Willingham hadn't seemed to notice.

Stephanie got into her rented Ford, snapped the door locks, and turned on the engine. She checked the traffic in both directions, then pulled out of the parking lot.

She felt badly, leaving this way, never even saying goodbye or thank-you to Annie, but if she'd done either, Annie would have wanted to know why she was leaving so early, and what could she possibly have said?

I'm leaving because there's a man here who's been coming on to me.

Oh, yeah. That would have gone over big, considering that Annie had clearly hoped for exactly that to happen.

Stephanie frowned as she approached the on-ramp to the highway. She slowed the car, checked right, then left, and carefully accelerated.

If Annie only knew. If she only had an idea of what had gone on. The way David Chambers had looked at her, as if he wanted to—to—

He'd even said as much! Oh, if Annie only knew. If she knew that he'd told her he wanted to make love to her, that it was what she wanted, too.

Stephanie's heart did a quick flip-flop.

How dare he?

"How *dare* he?" she muttered.

She hadn't wanted any such thing. Never. Not with this—this self-satisfied, smug cowboy or with any other man. She shuddered. Not since Avery—not since her husband had...

Was that the airport exit? Had she missed it? There was a sign, but she'd gone by too fast to read it.

Too fast?

She frowned, looked down at the speedometer. Sixty. She was doing sixty? The speed limit in this state was fifty-five—she'd made a point of asking at the car rental counter at the airport. She never drove above the limit. Never. Not when she was back home in Georgia; not when she was on vacation.

Stephanie eased her foot from the pedal and the speedometer needle dropped back to a safe and sane fifty. Not that she'd been on many vacations. Actually, there'd been just the one, to Cape Cod. She really hadn't much wanted to go. It had been her attorney's idea.

''You need to get away,'' he'd said firmly, making it sound as if he were concerned for her welfare when really he'd just wanted her out of the way. But she'd been too naive to figure that out, so she'd agreed that, yes, a change of scene would do her good.

Of course, she hadn't wanted to be away from Paul for any great length of time. Not that her brother minded. He never seemed to notice anymore if she was there or not, but what did that matter? She would be there for him, always.

Always.

Just thinking about Paul drove all the idiocy about David Chambers from her head. She had more important things to worry about than her irrational response to a man with a sexy smile, knowing eyes and softly seductive words.

There! Straight ahead. The sign for the airport. And, beyond it, the exit ramp.

Stephanie slowed the car and put on her turn signal indicator. Carefully, she made her way toward Bradley and an earlier flight than she'd planned.

Surely, there would be one.

And after that…after that, there'd be Clare and the mess waiting for her at home, but what was the point in thinking about it now?

Things would work out. They just had to.

David smiled at the ticket clerk.

"Excellent," he said, and whipped his platinum charge card from his wallet.

"Which was it, sir? Window or aisle?"

"Aisle. Definitely. Even in first class, I can use the legroom."

The clerk smiled and batted her lashes at him. "Here you are, Mr. Chambers. Have a pleasant flight."

*   *   *

At the far end of the airport, Stephanie smiled and walked straight up to the ticket counter.

Seconds later her smile was gone. The only direct flight to Atlanta was the one she was ticketed on. It didn't leave for another four hours.

"I'm really sorry, Mrs. Willingham," the clerk said. "Unless..." The woman's fingers flew over the keyboard of her computer. "Let me just check something." She looked up, beaming happily. "I've got one seat on a flight to Washington, where I can put you on a connecting flight to Atlanta. It's a window seat—"

"That's fine."

"And it's in first class."

Stephanie hesitated, thinking of the cost, thinking, too, of how Avery would have laughed at her for hesitating, but you didn't change the habits of a lifetime that easily.

"Mrs. Willingham?" The clerk looked at the wall clock. "The plane's about to board."

Stephanie nodded. "I'll take it."

The flight was leaving from the opposite end of the terminal. It wasn't easy, rushing to get to it with high heels on.

Fortunately, she only had a garment bag to carry. That made things easier. Still, by the time she reached the gate, the lounge area was empty, and the attendant was just starting to shut the door that led to the boarding ramp.

"Wait," Stephanie cried.

The man turned, saw her hurrying toward him, and swung the door wide.

"Almost missed it," he sang out cheerfully as she shoved her boarding pass at him.

Stephanie ran down the ramp. The flight attendant smiled when she saw her coming.

"Almost missed it," she said as Stephanie stepped into the cabin and showed her her ticket stub. "Seat 3-A. Right over here, Mrs. Willingham. Why don't you give me your luggage and I'll tuck it away for you?"

Stephanie smiled her thanks, collapsed into her seat, and puffed out her breath.

Maybe it was just as well she'd had to go with such last-minute arrangements. She sighed, kicked off her shoes and stretched out her legs. She'd almost forgotten the luxury of first class. The soft, wide seat. The legroom. She turned her face to the window and shut her eyes. Mmm. This was exactly what she needed. Peace. Quiet. The opportunity to purge the arrogant, overbearing, disgustingly macho David Chambers from her mind...

The handsome, vital, sexy David Chambers from her mind.

She felt someone sit down in the seat beside her, heard the faint clink of a seat belt—heard a sharply indrawn breath.

"I don't believe it," a man's husky voice growled softly. "I leave my seat for two minutes, and I come back to this? Great God Almighty, I don't care how small the world is, I can't be this unlucky twice in one day."

Stephanie shot upright. It couldn't be... But it was. David was sitting in the aisle seat, looking at her with the same horrified disbelief she knew must be stamped across her face.

A sob of desperation burst from her throat, and she fumbled for the buckle of her seat belt.

"Stop the plane," she yelped, but it was too late.

Even as the words left her lips, the sleek jet lifted into the late afternoon sky and headed toward Washington, D.C.

CHAPTER FOUR

"Is THERE a problem, madam?"

David dragged his gaze from Stephanie's flushed face. The flight attendant stood over them, brows lifted, a concerned smile stapled to her lips.

Yes, he thought, reading her look, you're damned right there's a problem.

"Madam?"

"No," David said before Stephanie could answer. "There's no problem." He smiled, too, though it felt as if the attempt might crack his skin. "We're fine."

"We? *We?*" Stephanie fumbled madly with her seat belt. "There is no *we,* there's only me and this—this—" She glared at the attendant. "I want out of here!"

"Madam, if you would just calm down—"

"Either that or I want you to stop this plane. Take it back to—"

She gasped as David's hand clamped hard around her wrist. "You'll have to forgive my, ah, my wife's outburst."

"Your wife? Your *wife?* I am not—"

"She's taken all the courses. Fearless Flyers, Flight Without Fright...all of them." His tone was the embodiment of compassion and tolerance. "None of it's worked. She's still terrified of flying."

"That's a lie! It's all lies. I am not terrified of flying, and you are not my—"

"Darling." David turned his smile, feral and sharp with warning, in Stephanie's direction. "If you don't calm down, this charming young lady is going to have to tell the pilot that he's got a disturbed passenger on board and they'll call to have an ambulance waiting at the gate, just the same as last time. Isn't that right, miss?"

"Another lie! I am not—"

The breath hissed from Stephanie's lungs as David's fingers tightened around her wrist.

"You wouldn't want that to happen again, would you, darling?"

"I am not disturbed." Stephanie glared at the flight attendant. "Do I look disturbed? Do I?"

"No," the girl said in a way that clearly meant just the opposite. "But, ah, perhaps it would be best if I went up front and spoke with the captain."

"I'm certain that won't be necessary, miss." David looked at Stephanie again. "Darling," he said through his teeth, "I'm sure if you just calm down, you'll feel better. You don't want them to turn this plane around and take us back to Hartford, do you?''

Stephanie glared at him. He was right, and she knew it. She pulled her hand from his, turned away sharply and stared out the window.

''That's my girl.''

Stephanie swung toward him. ''I am most definitely *not* your…''

Her eyes met those of the flight attendant's. The only time Stephanie had seen a person look at another in quite the same fashion was the Fourth of July when Johnny Bullard had gotten drunk on White Lightning, pulled off all his clothes in the middle of the town square and announced to the gathering crowd that he was a rocket and he was going to blast off.

Oh, hell!

''Never mind,'' she said glumly, and turned her face to the window again.

''She'll be fine now,'' David said.

''Are you sure, sir? Because if there's going to be a problem—''

''There won't be, will there, dearest?''

Not until I figure out a way to get even, there won't be…

''Darling?'' David said. ''Will there be a problem?''

"No," Stephanie said coldly.

The attendant produced another thousand-watt smile. "Thank you, ma'am. Now, if you'd just buckle your seat belt? I'm afraid we've been told to expect some bumpy weather ahead."

"For the rest of the passengers, or just for the man sitting next to me?" Stephanie said sweetly.

"I'm sure this young lady doesn't want to get in the middle of our private little spat, darling." David leaned toward her, a warning light glinting in his eyes. "Would you like me to buckle your belt for you?"

"Not unless you want to lose both your hands," she said through her teeth as she snapped the edges of the seat belt together.

David looked up at the flight attendant. "Thank you for your concern. You can see that we're fine now, Miss—" He peered at her badge, then gave her a dazzling smile. "Miss Edgecomb."

Stephanie watched bitterly as the girl's knees almost buckled under the sexy force of that smile. Oh, if she only knew what a no-good, scheming rat David Chambers really was.

"Yes, sir," Miss Edgecomb said. "And if I can be of any further help..."

"Of course. I'll be sure and let you know."

She bent down and whispered something. Stephanie couldn't hear it and didn't much want to, but David's easy laughter set her teeth on edge. She swung toward him, glaring, once they were alone.

"That was certainly a charming scene you orchestrated."

David put his seat back. "I'd love to take credit for it," he said, shutting his eyes, "but you're the one deserves all the applause."

"You have her convinced I'm crazy!"

"Sorry, but you get full credit for that, too."

"What did she say to you just now? Did she offer her sympathy?"

"She said that it might be a good idea to tank you up to the eyeballs with medication next time we fly."

"How generous of her."

"I said I hadn't known you'd intended to fly with me this time, that your presence had come as a delightful surprise."

"Oh, yeah. I'll just bet it did!"

"Meaning?"

"Do me a favor, Mr. Chambers. Don't try and play me for a fool. Do you really think I'm so naive I wouldn't realize you'd followed me?"

David blinked open his eyes. "Maybe she's right. Maybe you *are* nuts. Either that, or you're the most conceited broad I ever met."

"I am neither crazy nor conceited. And I no more appreciate being called a 'broad' than I appreciate having you follow me!"

"You really believe that?"

"No," she purred, "of course not. You just happened to turn up at the same airport, at the same time, and got yourself ticketed on the very same flight and, oh, yes, what an extra little coincidence, you ended up sitting right beside me." Stephanie sniffed. "I repeat, sir, I am neither naive, nor am I a fool."

David sighed. Her accent was back, that faint softening of vowels along with the way she had of addressing him as "sir" when the truth was the name she really had in mind was a lot less polite. She'd blushed the last time he'd commented on her drawl, which certainly made it worth commenting on again.

But he wasn't about to encourage this conversation. It had been a long day, he was tired, his disposition was so frazzled it was damn near nonexistent. The last thing he felt like doing was stepping into the ring and going another round with Stephanie Willingham, no matter how intriguing the possibility.

"The very idea," she muttered, "thinking you could pull off something so downright crass!"

"Mrs. Willingham," he said wearily, "I suggest again, calm down."

"What did you do, sir? Tail me from the country club?"

"Tail you?" He laughed in a way that sent the color sweeping back into Stephanie's face. "I think you've seen one bad detective movie too many."

"I do not watch detective movies, sir, bad or otherwise."

"Listen, Mrs. Willingham—"

"Dammit! Stop calling me that!"

David's mouth twisted. "Okay, Scarlett. Whatever you say. You want to think I came after you? Think it. Think whatever you like, so long as you shut up."

"It was sheer good fortune that placed you in the seat beside me. Is that what you'd like me to believe?"

"No, I would not."

She shot him a quick, mirthless smile. "That's something, anyway."

David opened one eye and looked in Stephanie's direction. "Good fortune would have put me down in the cargo hatch. Strapped to the wing. If luck had anything to do with this, I'd be on a rocket to Mars. I'd be anywhere but here."

"Ha."

He stabbed impatiently at the button that returned his seat to an upright position. There was to be no rest for him, he could see that. Bad weather was closing in on all sides: from the woman beside him, who obviously wasn't going to shut up until they touched down in D.C., and from the oily gray clouds that surrounded the plane. They were headed into a storm. The plane was starting to buck like a horse with a burr under its saddle. It was, he thought grimly, an apt metaphor for how he felt.

"Try and get this into your head, Scarlett," he growled, leaning toward her. "I'm just about as thrilled with our seating arrangements as you are, so here's my suggestion. Shut that pretty mouth of yours. That way, we can forget all about each other. How's that sound?"

"Like the first intelligent thing you've said," Stephanie said, fixing him with a cold look.

She folded her hands and did her best to ignore him. But it wasn't easy. How could she ignore him when each time the plane took a bone-jarring bounce—something it was doing with unsettling frequency—his shoulder brushed against hers? The scent of his cologne was annoying, too, that clean, outdoorsy aroma of leather and pine forests. She glanced at him from the corner of her eye. His profile might have been sculpted in granite. That chiseled forehead. That straight nose. The firm, full mouth and the strong, square chin.

His chin had stubble on it. So did his jaw. Her fingers curled into her palms. She could almost imagine the feel of that stubble under the soft stroke of her hand…

Stephanie sat up straighter.

"There must be an empty seat somewhere on this plane," she said angrily.

"No."

"No? No? What do you mean, no?"

"I mean exactly what I said. The plane's as full as a can of sardines."

"Wonderful." Stephanie folded her arms.

"Look, we'll be in Washington soon. And then we'll never have to set eyes on each other again."

"Thank goodness for that."

"I'm not going to argue, Scarlett." David shot her a quick look. "Frankly, I can hardly wait to be rid of you."

"Oh, do be frank, sir," Stephanie said coldly. "Considering that you've spent the afternoon being the soul of discretion, I imagine that a little frankness would be soothing."

David gritted his teeth. What in hell had he done to deserve being saddled with such an impossible woman? She was gorgeous, yes, maybe even more now than before, where their surroundings demanded she at least try to maintain a civilized veneer. Her eyes were bright, her cheeks red, and her breathing had quickened so that her breasts rose and fell in a way a man couldn't possibly ignore. She was clever, too, and more than willing to stand up to him despite her look of fragility.

But she was impossible. Stephanie Willingham was a short-tempered, sharp-tongued, opinionated hellion. She wouldn't appreciate the comparison, but she reminded him of a wild mare he'd brought down from the high summer pastures a couple of years before.

The filly had been a beautiful animal, with fine bones, a soft, silky mane and tail—and the disposition of a wildcat. His men had tried everything to gentle her, but nothing had worked. They'd have to break her spirit, his foreman finally said…but David had refused to let that happen. He'd wanted the horse to accept the saddle, and him, not out of fear but out of desire.

So he'd taken up the challenge. He'd talked softly to the filly, offered her treats from his hand despite the sharp nips she'd given him. He'd stroked her neck, the rare occasions she'd permitted it. And at last, early one morning, instead of greeting him with wildly rolling eyes and bared teeth, the mare had come slowly to the fence, buried her velvet muzzle in the crook of his shoulder and trembled with pleasure as he touched her.

"Well?"

He looked up. Stephanie was glaring at him in defiance. Somewhere along the line, her dark hair had begun to escape its neat, nape-of-the-neck knot. Strands of it curled lightly against her ears and throat.

I could tame you, he thought, and he felt the swift surge of hot blood race through his veins.

"Well, what?" he said very softly.

Something in his voice, in the way his blue eyes were boring into her, made Stephanie's pulse beat quicken.

"Nothing," she said.

"Come on, Miss Scarlett, don't chicken out now." David smiled silkily. "You were going to tell me something, and I'd like to hear it."

Don't say anything, a tiny voice within Stephanie's head whispered. He's baiting you, and he's dangerous. You're playing out of your league here....

A tingle of excitement danced over her skin.

"Only," she said, carefully and very deliberately, "only that you're the most arrogant, ill-mannered, self-centered male I've ever had the misfortune to—"

She gasped as his hand closed around her wrist.

"Am I?"

His voice was low and rough. Stephanie felt as if she could hardly breathe. Her thoughts flew back to when her grandmother had still been alive. She'd been sent to live with her one summer. She was three, four, too young, anyway, to know the difference between honey that came from a jar and the stuff that oozed from a broken, bee-laden comb lying beneath Gramma's old pin oak.

"Leave it be, child," Gramma had cried as she'd reached for the comb, but Stephanie had already brought it to her mouth. The moment was forever frozen in time: the candied kiss of the welling honey, and then the fierce, painful sting of the bee.

She thought of it now, that dizzying combination of sweetness and danger, as David bent toward her. Should she force herself to face him down...or should she leap from her seat and run for her life, never mind that the plane was dipping and rising like a roller coaster, or that the flight attendant would probably call ahead and have the men in the white coats waiting.

No. Why should she run? There was nothing to be afraid of. What could happen here, in this public place?

Anything. The word whispered through her like a hot wind.

David's eyes smoldered with heat. She could almost scent his anger on the air. No, she thought, her heart giving another giddy kick, not his anger. His masculinity. His awareness of her not as a foe but as a woman.

The plane was carrying them into a velvet darkness. As if from a great distance, she heard the disembodied voice of the captain requesting that all passengers be sure they were buckled in. The cabin lights blinked on and off, on and off, and she caught a glimpse of lightning zigzagging like flame outside the window.

Somewhere in the cabin behind her, a woman's voice rose in fear. Stephanie knew she ought to be afraid, too, of the storm raging just beyond the fragile shell of their aircraft, but the only storm she could think about was the one that had been building between David and her from the moment they'd met.

He undid his seat belt, his gaze never leaving her face. A soft whimper rose in her throat and it took all her strength to suppress it.

''Do you like playing games, Scarlett?'' He moved closer; his thumb rolled across her bottom lip, the tip of it just insinuating itself into her mouth. He tasted of heat, of salt. Of passion.

"That's what we've been doing all day, isn't it? Playing games." His gaze fell to her mouth; she felt the hungry weight of it, like a caress, before his eyes met hers again. "No more games, Stephanie," he said gruffly, and he kissed her.

She made no sound, moved not an inch. But the moan she'd managed to hold back moments ago slipped through the kiss. She felt a tremor pass through him and then he thrust one hand into her hair, tipped her head back, and parted her lips with his.

There was no time to think. All she could do was react—and respond. Stephanie whimpered softly, wound her arms around David's neck, and opened her mouth to his kiss.

The lights in the cabin blinked out. Blackness engulfed them. The plane lifted, then dropped as if there were a hole in the sky. They were alone on the dark, wild sea of the heavens, and at its mercy.

Stephanie wasn't afraid. She felt the strength of David's arms as they encircled her, felt the racing pound of his heart against hers, and when his hand slid under the jacket of her suit and cupped her breast, she cried out in pleasure.

"Yes," he whispered. "Oh, yes."

She felt the nip of his teeth. Her head fell back as he pressed his lips to her throat and when he brought her hand to him, settled it against the powerful thrust of his arousal, she arched against him.

This was wrong. It was insane. She knew that, knew it well. But to stop what she felt, what David was making her feel, was impossible. His hunger was fierce, but so was hers. She had to assuage it, had to give in to it, had to touch and be touched....

The lights in the cabin blazed on. The plane rocked one last time, then settled onto a steady course.

It was all Stephanie needed to return her to reality.

She gave a muffled cry and tried to break free, but David wouldn't let her. He clasped her face between his hands, his mouth hot and demanding on hers...and despite everything, the cabin lights, and the voice of the captain assuring the passengers that they were okay, despite all that, she almost gave herself up again to the passion, the intoxication of this stranger's kiss.

''No!'' Stephanie slammed her fists against his chest, tore her mouth from his. ''Stop it,'' she said, her voice trembling, and David blinked his eyes, like a man awakening from a deep dream.

He drew back and stared into the flushed face of this woman he'd met only hours before. Her eyes were huge and glazed; her mouth was swollen from his kisses and her hair had come undone so that dark strands curled lightly around her face.

''You're despicable,'' she hissed as she twisted away from him, as far as she could get.

A muscle knotted in David's cheek. He sat back, his hands curled tightly around the armrests of his seat. Despicable? Crazy might be a better word.

''Mrs. Willingham…'' he said.

Mrs. Willingham? He really *was* crazy, addressing a woman he'd damn near ravaged with such formality. And what was he going to say to her? I'm sorry? Hell, he was not. Not sorry, not apologetic, not any of those things because she'd wanted what had happened as much as he had.

''Ladies and gentlemen.'' The amplified voice of the flight attendant interrupted his thoughts. ''The captain has asked me to tell you that we are on our approach to Dulles and we should be on the ground in just a few minutes.''

A thin cheer of relief rose from the passengers. David felt like cheering, too, but it had nothing to do with having survived the storm. He'd survived something else entirely.

He was a man who'd known his fair share of women. Okay, more than his fair share, some would say. He was not a stranger to the fever that could flare like wildfire between two consenting adults.

But nothing like this had ever happened to him before. If the lights hadn't come on, if Stephanie hadn't stopped him, he'd have taken her there, in the darkness. In the hot little universe they'd created. He'd have ripped off her panties, buried himself deep in her heat until—until…

He'd been out of control, and he knew it. And it scared the hell out of him.

Life—his life—was all about control. Control of the self. It was how he'd gone from being a kid enduring life in a foster home to a man with a law degree and a well-regarded practice. He'd only made that one slip, when he'd let himself think he was in love, let himself trust a woman who wasn't to be trusted.…

The plane touched down with a thump. There was scattered applause, a few whistles, but David was already on his feet, reaching for his garment bag, making his way up the aisle to the door.

"Sir? Mr. Chambers?" The flight attendant smiled and sent a darting look over his shoulder. "Isn't your wife—"

"She isn't my wife," David said fiercely. "She isn't anything, not to me."

He left the flight attendant's voice behind him, left everything behind him. Whatever it was that had happened to him in that airplane cabin was over. And he sure as hell was never going to think about it again.

CHAPTER FIVE

THERE were few certainties in life.

Stephanie knew that. It was, in fact, the very first certainty.

The others ranged from the sublime to the ridiculous.

For instance, she knew that a pair of cardinals would rebuild the old nest deep within the shelter of the rhododendron outside the back door, come every spring.

They were there now, on this bright, warm morning, the male in his bright plumage chirping encouragement to the female as she flew off for more twigs.

"I don't know that it's the same pair, ma'am," the gardener had said when he'd found her watching them that first spring, seven long years ago. "Might be younguns of the first two what built that nest."

It didn't matter. If it was a new generation doing the building, that only made what was happening all the sweeter. Somebody, even if that somebody had wings and feathers, believed in home and family.

And then there were the other constants, the ones that were not so pleasant.

The way the good townsfolk of Willingham Corners looked at her whenever she drove into town. Not that it was very different from how they'd always looked at her, the men with sly smiles that made her skin crawl, the women with condemnation tightening their mouths.

Well, that was surely going to change, and soon. Smirks would replace the smiles, and the looks of condemnation would be replaced by ones that said morality had, at last, triumphed.

Stephanie glanced at the dining room table, and the letter lying on it. Oh, yes. Just wait until the town heard about that.

They'd probably celebrate.

Stephanie Willingham, Mrs. Avery Willingham, was going to lose the roof over her head and the ground under her feet. She was going to lose everything.

Everything—including the one thing that mattered, that she had bartered her soul to possess.

She should have known Avery would renege on his promise. His word had never been any good—another of life's little certainties, Stephanie thought with a bitter smile, but one she'd only learned after they'd made their unholy bargain.

There wasn't even any point in telling herself that the documents Avery's sister had produced were forgeries. It would have given Avery as much pleasure to have arranged the situation as it had given Clare to hint at it. It was the cruelty of the thing that had convinced her, the "joint tenancy" provisions carefully devised to make Clare Avery's heir—and to leave Stephanie with absolutely nothing.

Oh, yes, the documents were legitimate. It was Avery's final gift—which only emphasized the last certainty.

Men were a bunch of double-dealing bastards.

They'd lie to get what they wanted and then fix it so that their promises were worth about as much as they were.

Stephanie put her hand to her forehead. Except for Paul. Paul was different, and not just because he was her brother. Paul was kind, and caring; he'd always been there for her, when she was little. No one else had been. Not her father, whom she'd never known. Not her mother, who'd wandered out of her children's lives like a wisp of smoke.

And not Avery. God, certainly not Avery.

Stephanie put her back to the window and looked down blindly into the cup of rapidly cooling coffee cradled between her palms. Avery, with his talk of being the father she'd never had. With his compassionate gifts—the food basket on Thanksgiving, the visits to the specialists for Paul, the big box of books she'd hungered for but couldn't afford to buy. And then the greatest gift of all, the one she'd believed would be the start of a better life, for her and for Paul...a year's tuition for Miss Carol's Secretarial School.

"It's too much, Mr. Willingham," Stephanie had said. "I can't let you do this."

"Sure you can, darlin'." Avery had put a beefy arm around her shoulders in fatherly fashion. "You learn to type, take dictation, an' I'll give you a job, workin' for me."

Working for him, Stephanie thought, and shuddered.

Oh, how he'd hooked her. Set out a lure she couldn't resist and reeled her in like a fish all ready for the skillet.

How could she have been so naive? So stupid? So pathetically, painfully dumb?

Not that the answers mattered anymore. It was true, fate had intervened. Paul had become more and more withdrawn but still, it was she who'd agreed to make a contract with the devil.

There was no one to blame but herself…

Just as she was to blame for what had happened two weeks ago, on what should have been a pleasant, peaceful Sunday afternoon.

Stephanie shut her eyes against the humiliating memory. That she'd let a stranger do those things to her—that she'd let *any* man do those things to her—was inconceivable. None of it made sense. She knew what men were and what they wanted. What they always wanted, whether they were old and fat, like Avery, or young and handsome, like David Chambers.

Sex. That was what men wanted. And sex was—it was…

Stephanie shuddered again, despite the warmth of the morning sun on her shoulders. Sweat. Grasping hands. Hot breath on your face and wet lips smothering you, and the feel of bile rising in the back of your throat…

Except, it hadn't been like that with David. When he'd kissed her. Touched her. Cupped her breast and made her moan. She could still remember the taste of him, the feel of his mouth, warm against hers, his kiss hinting at pleasures she'd never imagined…

"Missus Willingham?"

Stephanie spun around. Mrs. Cross stood in the doorway. The straw hat she wore for marketing days was on her head; her suitcase was in her hand.

"I'm leavin'," she said coldly. "Thought I'd let you know."

Stephanie nodded. "I understand. I'm sorry I haven't been able to pay you the last few weeks, but—"

"Wouldn't stay under this roof, money or no money," the housekeeper said. "Town knows what you are now, missus, what with Mr. Avery fixin' things for all to see."

Coffee sloshed over the rim of Stephanie's cup and onto her hand, but she didn't so much as blink.

"I'll send you a check for what I owe you, Mrs. Cross." Her voice was clear and steady. She'd be damned—*damned*—if she'd break down now. "You may have to wait for your money, but you'll get it all, I promise."

"Don't want nothin' from you, missus."

Mrs. Cross turned on her heel and marched off. Stephanie didn't move as she listened to the housekeeper's footsteps stomp the length of the marbled hall, but after the front door slammed shut, she pulled a chair out from the table and sank down into it.

"And a good thing you don't, Mrs. Cross," she whispered shakily, "because I don't have anything left to give."

Her eyes burned with unshed tears. She blinked hard, then drew a deep breath.

"All right," she said briskly, and scrubbed her hands over her face.

What was done, was done. There was no sense in brooding over things, or in playing a game of "What if?" What was it her mother used to say? It was hard to remember; it seemed such a long, long time ago...

"No use cryin' over spilled milk, Steffie. Just mop it up an' get on with your life."

The advice still held. She had to get on with her life, put aside what the town thought, what Avery had done...put aside, as well, all memories of whatever it was that had happened between her and David Chambers. He wasn't even worth thinking about. For all his looks and money and charm, he was nothing but another member of the brotherhood, a lying, sneaking, self-centered, testosterone-impaired, no-account rat—and the only good news about that Sunday was that it was over, and she'd never see the man's face again.

Stephanie swiped her hand across her eyes one last time, then reached for the letter from Clare's attorneys. Not that she needed to read it. She'd paced the floor with it the last ten days; its message was embedded in her brain.

Dear Mrs. Willingham: Please be advised that it is the wish of our client, Clare Willingham, that you vacate her property no later than Friday the thirteenth.

"Such a propitious date, don't you think?" Clare had purred, when she'd phoned to have the pleasure of delivering the news, firsthand.

Stephanie's throat constricted. She cleared it, then read the next sentence aloud into the silence of the room.

"Please be advised that the stipend paid to your account will cease as of that date, as well."

That was the phrase that had made her begin to tremble.

That was when she'd known she was lost.

She'd tried fighting it. Months ago, as soon as Clare had started dropping hints that Stephanie's days at Seven Oaks were limited, she'd gone to see Amos Turner, who had a law office in town.

"I don't give a damn about the house," she'd told him. "I only want what's rightfully mine. Avery promised to put a specified amount of money into my checking account each month."

"How much?" Turner asked with an oily smile.

Stephanie took a deep breath. "Twenty-five hundred dollars."

The lawyer smiled. "My, my, my," he purred, "that surely is a lot of money for a man to provide his wife as an allowance."

"It wasn't an allowance."

"No? What was it then, my dear?"

Payment. Payment for selling her soul...

"I don't see how that's germane, Mr. Turner," she said coolly.

Turner's beady eyes glistened. "Must be nice, havin' such a value put on yourself," he said, tilting back his chair so that his fat belly protruded like an island in a sea of shiny black worsted.

Stephanie flushed but she refused to give an inch. What was the point? The town had made up its mind about her a long time ago.

"Bet you earned every bit of that money, too," he'd said, and she'd looked him squarely in the eye and assured him that he was damned right. She had.

Such brave talk, she thought now. Her mouth trembled. And so useless. Turner had folded like an accordion after a meeting with Clare and, she had no doubt, with Clare's checkbook. Judge Parker had proved no obstacle to the proceedings, either.

And so it was over. She had nothing. No roof over her head, no money—and no way to pay for Paul's care.

Panic sent her heart thump-thumping in her chest.

There had to be something she could do. She was Avery's widow, wasn't she? A widow had certain rights. Sure, the Willinghams owned this town, but they didn't rule the world.

Stephanie rose to her feet. She'd met an attorney once, at one of the dinner parties she'd hosted for Avery. The man didn't practice here, he practiced...where? Washington. That was it. What was his name?

Hustle? Fussell?

Russell. That was it. Jack Russell, like the breed of dog. She'd blurted that out when they'd been introduced, and Avery's arm had tightened around her waist and he'd pinched her, where no one could see. She'd tried to stammer out an apology but Russell had bowed over her hand and assured her, in a drawl thicker than hers, that he had no objection to being compared to a handsome, feisty little terrier, especially when the comparison was made by such a beautiful woman.

Russell had smiled at her the entire evening. Not the way other men did. His smile had been kind, and generous, and tinged, she'd thought, with a little sadness.

"If this old ogre ever mistreats you, my dear," he'd said, kissing her cheek at evening's end, when she and Avery stood at the ornate front door to bid their guests goodnight, "you just give me a call and I'll come to your rescue."

Avery had laughed in that way that made her skin crawl just to remember it.

"Not to worry," he'd said. "I know exactly how to treat a gal like this."

Stephanie blocked out the memory and hurried to the library, where Avery had kept his address book. There was no point in thinking about the past. It was the present that mattered and perhaps, if she were very, very lucky, Jack Russell could help her face that present and survive it.

She leafed through the book, found Russell's name and a Washington, D.C., telephone number.

"No use crying over spilled milk, Steffie," she whispered.

Then she took a deep breath and reached for the telephone.

Life had taught David a series of lessons.

Red wine was better than white.

Old Porsches were better than new ones.

Springtime in the nation's capitol was glorious.

But not this year, David thought as he sat with his back to his desk and stared out his office window.

The weather was mild. The sky was clear. The cherry blossoms were delivering their annual show, a little late, but the tourists didn't much care.

And still, he was in a foul mood.

Everybody had told him so, including his secretary. He'd never liked Miss Murchison much; he knew he'd hired her in a moment of weakness, when sympathy for her acne, mousy looks and weight problem had overruled logic.

What he hadn't counted on was that she couldn't type much faster than he could, or figure out how to turn on her computer without bringing down the entire system. She had her hat and coat on by five o'clock, promptly, and never mind that she'd known, right up front, that he sometimes would need her to put in an additional hour or so, for which her salary more than compensated.

Yesterday, after she'd taken an entire afternoon to type two letters and topped the day off by whining, ''But, Mr. Chambers, do you know what time it is?'' when, at twenty minutes of five, he'd asked her to please retype one of the letters she'd managed to get chocolate stains on, he'd finally exploded.

He said that he knew exactly what time it was. It was time for her to find a new job. Time for her to inflict herself on somebody else…

David shut his eyes and groaned.

So much for doing things that seemed right at the time you did them. He'd ended up with a weeping Miss Murchison and a knot in his belly.

''Don't cry, for God's sake,'' he'd said helplessly, and then he'd done his best to soothe her hurt feelings by writing out a check for three months' severance pay and handed it over along with a rambling tale about his rotten mood being caused by a headache that simply refused to go away. Miss Murchison, who'd managed a swift recovery once she had his check firmly in her hand, had sniffed and said that any man who'd had a rotten headache for two weeks' straight was a man with a problem.

She was right. He *did* have a problem, and its name was Stephanie Willingham. The woman was in his head, night and day, and wasn't that ridiculous? Okay, so he'd been attracted to her. Okay, so he'd come on to her…

David groaned again and slumped back in his chair. To hell with all that. He'd behaved like a jerk, and he knew it. Kissing her in that airplane. Touching her. Damn near ravishing her… Who knew what he'd have done if the lights hadn't come back on when they did?

Why? Because she was good-looking? So were half the women on the planet. So were all the women in his little black book, and he'd never made a fool of himself with any of them.

Maybe he needed a break. Yes, that was it. This town was great. He loved its pace, its excitement, the realization that he was practicing high-powered law in the very heart of the western world, but sometimes it got to be too much. The crowds. The cars. The day that began at six and ended after midnight, if you added in the dinners and parties and charity affairs he had to attend.

''We work our tails off,'' Jack Russell had told him when David had come on board more than a dozen cherry-blossom seasons ago, and the esteemed law firm of Russell, Russell and Hanley had become Russell, Russell, Hanley and Chambers. ''But if you like living on the edge, David, you'll love it here.''

David had smiled and said he was sure he would.

''No place prettier than D.C. in the springtime,'' Jack had said as David's gaze went to the cherry trees out on the street, and David had smiled again and asked Jack if he'd ever seen Wyoming this time of year.

"No," Jack had replied. "Bet it's all snow and cold winds."

Snow, David thought, staring out the window. Probably. The mountains ringing his ranch would still bear their winter cloaks…and yet, if he saddled a horse and went riding, he knew he'd see the signs of rebirth all around. The rosy tinge birch branches get when the sap begins to flow. Green shoots seeking the sun's warmth where the snow had blown away. Calves butting their heads against their mothers' bellies and colts, still gawky on their long, ungainly legs…

"Hell," David muttered, and swiveled his chair back toward his desk.

Sitting here and staring out the windows was not going to get any work done. And he had a lot of work to do. Tons of it, from the look of his appointment book, with "hire a secretary" right on top.

It was just that he was in the darkest mood. The Cooper wedding had taken place two weeks ago but the memory of Stephanie Willingham wouldn't go away. And never mind all that stuff he'd been telling himself about damn near ravishing her. Who was he trying to kid? The widow Willingham, she of the icy words and the hot mouth, had sizzled as soon as he'd looked at her.

And when he'd touched her—when he'd touched her…

David mouthed an oath, rose to his feet and stalked across his office. There was a carafe of fresh coffee on an antique mahogany sideboard and it took him a couple of seconds to remember that this was not the pale slop Miss Murchison had passed off as coffee but a pot he'd brewed for himself. He poured a cup, took a sip, and plunked himself down on one of a pair of small leather sofas.

Enough of this crap. He'd been dragging his butt for days, alternately chewing himself out for the idiotic way he'd behaved with Stephanie and fantasizing over what might have happened if they hadn't been in a plane but in his town house. It was time to move on to something else.

What he needed was a good, swift dose of reality. A workout in his gym. A couple of games of racquetball, maybe, or half an hour trading jabs with a punching bag…

Or a weekend at home.

David put down his cup, rose and strolled to the window. Yes. That would do it. A couple of afternoons spent digging fence posts or stringing wire after the damages of the winter would put him on track again. Hard work and sweat went a long way toward reminding a man of what really mattered in the overall scheme of things. That conviction had taken him home nearly every weekend after he'd first come east to practice law.

Reality, he had known instinctively, would always lie to the west, in Wyoming.

It was unfortunate that his wife—his exwife—had figured it to be just the opposite. The real world, Krissie had insisted, was in Georgetown. The cocktail parties and dinners, the tweedy weekends spent at elegant old homes in the Virginia countryside—all the stuff that made him wince, made her smile.

Krissie's idea of a cozy evening at home involved twenty or thirty of her closest friends.

A muscle knotted in David's cheek. It had not been that way when they'd been dating.

Back then, she'd professed to love the things he loved. The ranch, and riding out to the purple hills. Quiet meals by the fireside and afterward, soft music on the CD player, and freshly made popcorn...and long hours spent in each other's arms.

It was going to be like a fairy tale. One man, one woman. One love, forever after.

What a fool he'd been. Women said what a man wanted to hear when they were setting the snare that would trap him. His wife had lied about everything, what she liked, what she disliked...

About fidelity.

He'd tolerated all of it. Everything—right up until the day he'd come home early and found her in bed with another man. That he hadn't killed the son of a bitch and thrown Krissie into the street bare-ass naked was less a reflection of his forbearance than an indication of how little she'd meant to him by then.

The divorce had been swift and nasty, the recovery lengthy and painful. But recover he had, and the lessons he'd learned had stuck.

Women were not to be trusted. They said one thing, meant another, and the man who didn't keep that always, *always,* in mind deserved what he got.

David smiled. That wasn't to say that women didn't have their uses. He liked women. He liked the way they sounded, and the way they smelled. He liked the softness of their laughter, the curved lushness of their bodies...

Stephanie had a lush body. Her skin had been soft as silk, hot as flame under his hands. And the taste of her mouth...he'd never known a taste like it. So honeyed. So sweet. So exciting...

David swung away from the window, his breathing harsh. What in hell was he doing, thinking about her? It was crazy. Crazy! The world was filled with women. Obliging women, who didn't say "no" when they meant "yes"—and yet his thoughts were possessed by one who did just that.

Stephanie.

He'd even phoned Annie Cooper, late last week, and after a few minutes of inconsequential chitchat, he'd brought Stephanie's name into the conversation, asked Annie about her, then braced himself for the teasing he'd figured he was sure to get. But Annie had seemed preoccupied. She'd said she didn't know Stephanie very well, only that she was a widow whose husband had died fairly recently.

"Is it important?" she'd said, adding that if it was, she could always give Stephanie a call.

"No," David had said quickly, "no, it's not important at all."

Annie, completely out of character, had let the subject go. He'd hung up the phone, reached for his Rolodex file, had his hand on the card of the private investigator the firm sometimes used before he'd realized that he was behaving like a certifiable nutcase.

David sighed, sat down behind his desk and picked up a pencil. Instead of reaching for the private investigator's card, he'd reached for his own private address book. He'd made some phone calls, then spent the next few evenings pleasantly, in the company of half a dozen bright, beautiful females. He'd taken them out, he'd taken them home—one at a time, he thought, with a little smile...

His smile faded. And then, despite the promises in their eyes, he'd kissed them gently, eased their arms from his neck, said goodnight and gone home, alone, to lie in his bed and dream of a woman he would never see again, never wanted to see again...

"Hell," he said through his teeth, and snapped the pencil in two.

"Careful, lad. Got to watch that temper."

David jerked his head up. Jack Russell stood in the doorway, smiling, thumbs tucked into the pockets of his old-fashioned vest.

"Jack." David mustered a smile. "Good morning."

"It is that." Jack strolled into the room, sat down on the chair across from David's desk, and glanced at the window. "Though, I must say, the cherry blossoms aren't all they should be this year."

"Nothing is all it should be," David said flatly. Jack shot him a quizzical look, and he managed another smile. "What can I do for you this morning?"

"Well, for openers, you can tell me where you were last night."

"Where I was last..." David puffed out his breath. "The Weller cocktail party! Jack, I'm sorry."

"That's all right. I made your apologies to our host and hostess, and told them you were up to your neck in work."

"I owe you one."

Jack chuckled. "You owe me several. I've protected your *gluteus maximus* more than once in the past couple of weeks."

"Yeah. Well, you know how it is. I've been...busy."

"Preoccupied, might be a better word. Something on your mind?"

"Listen, just because I blew a couple of appointments..."

"Six," Jack said, ticking them off on his fingers. "Three dinners, one round of drinks, one embassy do and that charity auction last weekend."

"I told you," David said brusquely, "I've been—"

"Busy. Yes, I know." Jack leaned back in his chair and crossed his arms. "Who's the lucky young woman?"

"The baloney I have to put up with," David said, forcing a smile to his lips, "because I'm the only bachelor around here..."

"And deservedly so, according to my better half. Mary says you need a wife."

David laughed. "You tell Mary that what I need is a secretary. Somebody to keep my appointments straight and type more than ten words a minute. I fired Murchison, did you hear?"

"Certainly. The other secretaries are taking up a collection."

"Yeah," David said, and sighed. "Well, I'm sure she'll appreciate the flowers, whatever it is they send her. Tell them they can count on me for my share."

Jack chuckled. "The collection's for you, David. They figure you deserve a bouquet for tolerating her as long as you did." Jack pursed his lips. "So, now what?"

"Well, I've arranged for a temp. Next week, I'll phone that agency we always use..."

"I meant, what about you? Murchison's not around to irritate you and everybody else. So, now will you stop going around looking like a hound dog with a tick under its tail?"

David grinned and leaned back in his chair. "Uh-oh."

"Uh-oh, what?"

"When you start tossing out the down-home maxims—even though you haven't lived in that little dot on the map you call home for three decades—it's always a bad sign. Means you're going to tell me something you figure I won't want to hear."

"Four decades," the older man said modestly, "and Macon, Georgia, is hardly a dot on the map. Still, roots is roots, as my ol' granpappy used to say."

"Your 'ol' granpappy' was a supreme court justice."

Jack mimed being shot in the heart. "A direct hit! Nonetheless, roots is—"

"—Roots. Yeah. I know." David's smile tilted. "To tell the truth, I'm pretty much overdosed on things south of the Mason-Dixon line, as of late."

"Is that why you've been as grouchy as a boll weevil at harvesttime the past couple of weeks?"

"Jack…"

"Okay, okay, I'll keep my store of country wisdom to myself."

"Good. Now, what is it you need to tell me that I'm not going to like?"

Jack leaned forward, his hands on his knees. "You recall a situation last year? The Anderson mess, where the old man died intestate and suddenly three cousins turned up with three different wills?''

''Sure. We represented the old guy's son, and we won. Don't tell me one of the cousins hired himself another lawyer!''

''No, no. It's just that this reminds me a bit of that situation. Man kicks off. Leaves behind a wife but no will, and then it turns out he held his entire estate in joint tenancy with his sister, who now has, of course, full rights of survivorship.''

''Was he trying to defraud his widow?''

Jack shook his head. ''The court says no. The widow ends up without a dime.''

''Ouch,'' David said, picturing a white-haired old lady turned out onto the streets.

''Ouch, indeed. I just got the call a little while ago, from the wife of the dead man. He was an old friend… Well, no. He wasn't a friend. Not at all. An acquaintance, you might say, from a town twenty, twenty-five miles from Macon.''

''And?''

''And, she's penniless. The widow's not surprised—says she should have figured he'd leave her nothing.''

David's eyebrows rose. ''No love lost in the relationship, I gather?''

''None.'' Jack rose to his feet and paced around the office, his hands in his pockets. ''I only met the lady once, years ago. Can't say I remember much about the meeting, except that she was a tiny little thing, seemed kind of sad.''

''She wants you to represent her?''

''Well, she asked if I'd look things over, see if she's not at least entitled to the monthly stipend her husband had been giving her. I didn't ask too many questions because I could see there might be a conflict of interest. You see, the dead man's sister was a school friend of Mary's. Same sorority, all that nonsense. Bottom line is that I know Clare rather well.'' Jack smiled. ''I don't like her, but I know her. So it's a problem.''

''Well, if you told that to the widow…''

''I told her this wasn't our cup of tea. Too messy. That's the truth, even if she had a chance of collecting something. Purty young thang from the backwoods—''

''The sister?''

''The widow.''

''Ah. I thought—well, from what you'd said, I assumed she was an older woman.''

''Young,'' Jack said. ''Very young. And more than pretty, as I recall. The story just about rocked the town. Beautiful girl—eighteen, nineteen years old—marries a man pushing sixty with both hands. Little lady's got swamp grass between her toes, he's from the town's first family.''

"She traded sex for money and power. Jack, that's the world's oldest profession. Second oldest, when people make it legit with a marriage license."

"The sister agrees. According to her, that's how the girl got a marriage ring on her finger. Bed for board, so to speak. But, says Sis, her brother wasn't a complete fool. He had no intention of providing for the girl beyond the here and now."

"The girl knew this?"

"She says she didn't. Says her hubby promised she'd be taken care of on a monthly basis, even after his death. She makes no bones about it, David. Kind of boasted to me that she'd insisted on it before she'd agree to marry him." Russell sat down again and crossed his legs. "Amazing, how cold-blooded some members of the so-called gentler sex can be, don't you think?"

David smiled tightly. "You're asking the wrong man that question, Jack."

"Sorry. I'd forgotten about that ex-wife of yours."

"Actually," David said, "I wasn't thinking of her at all. Well, go on. What is it you want from me? If it's my opinion, I don't see much of a chance for appeal or reversal. I suppose the girl

could sue, on the grounds that she's been de-
frauded of her rights to the estate.''

''She did, and the matter was decided against
her. She says she doesn't care about anything but
getting the monthly allowance her husband promised.''

''How much was it?''

''I don't know. I told you, I didn't ask too
many questions.''

''Well, whatever it was, fifty bucks or five hundred, I hope you told her the chances of that happening were slim to none.''

''I tried. But she started crying…''

David gave a wry smile. ''I'll bet.''

''I ended up promising I'd drive down and talk
to her—but then I realized how it would look,
considering my connections to the sister.''

''Damn right.''

''So,'' Jack said with a little smile, ''I'm asking you to do me a favor.''

''Jack, for heaven's sake…''

''It's not a big thing, David. Tomorrow's
Friday. You can fly to Atlanta in the morning, cab
to her house, be back before dinner.''

David frowned. ''You're leaving out the part
where I tell her not to be greedy, to be grateful
for the cash, jewelry, furs, whatever it is she's got
squirreled away.''

"Yes—except you might try doing it a little more gently."

"Why? To prove that lawyers have hearts?"

"That's a cold attitude, counselor."

"I'm feeling cold lately, Jack. And realistic."

"Look, we do pro bono work all the time, and that's all I'm suggesting here, an hour of free advice for a young woman who needs it. I have to admit, I feel sorry for her, even knowing she married for money."

"Sold herself, you mean."

"I suppose. Still, there's something about her. She has this vulnerability... What?" Jack said when David's mouth crooked in a half-smile.

"I knew a rancher once, said the same thing about a yearling grizzly cub just before it mauled him."

Jack laughed. "You see? Sometimes, nothing will do but a down-home sentiment." He sat down again and leaned forward. "Look, we both know the girl's a manipulative little gold digger, but she did keep her end of the deal, or so I gather. She stayed with Avery, right to the end."

"Such dedication," David said, folding his arms and tilting back in his chair.

"Don't be so hard-hearted. She's broke. She has no skills, no talents, well, none other than a secretarial course she took one time, before she married.'' Jack chuckled. ''There's an idea. Maybe you should offer her a job.''

''You're leaving a skill out, Jack. The one that got her a wedding ring.''

''Ah, yes.'' Russell gave a deep sigh. ''Amazing, what a man will put himself through, and all so he can get one particular woman into his bed.''

An image of Stephanie Willingham flashed through David's head.

''Amazing,'' he said coolly. ''Okay, I'll talk to her.''

''Thank you, David.''

''Don't thank me,'' David said, and smiled. ''I'll get my pound of flesh out of you, Jack. I'll make you go to the Sheratons' house party next weekend, instead of me.''

Jack laughed. ''Still running away from Mimi Sheraton? I wish I could oblige, but Mary's already made plans.''

''Terrific.''

''It will be. Just take out that little black book of yours and find yourself a playmate to take along for the weekend. That should stop Mimi.''

David snorted. Mimi Sheraton, daughter of a senator and married to a client who was husband number three—or was it four?—was stunning and about as subtle as a shark. Assertive women were fine—but one that groped you under the table while you were talking with her husband was definitely a turnoff.

"The only thing that would stop Mimi," he said, "would be the announcement of my death."

Jack laughed again. "Or of your engagement."

"Same thing."

The men smiled at each other, and then David reached for a pen and paper.

"Okay," he said. "I'll fly down to Atlanta tomorrow. No need to let grass grow on this."

"No need at all." Jack dug into his pocket and pulled out a slip of paper. "And I just happen to have the lady's address and phone number right here."

"All I need now," David said, glancing at the paper as he took it from his partner's outstretched hand, "is her name."

"Oh. Oh, right. I thought I'd… Her name is Willingham."

David stiffened, and his fingers tightened around the pen.

"It's what?"

"Willingham. Stephanie Willingham." Jack closed one eye in a slow, deliberate wink. "I don't know what today's terminology is but when I was a young and callow youth, we'd have described her as one hell of a piece of—"

"I know the phrase," David said. He tried to smile but from the look on the older man's face, he suspected he wasn't succeeding. "Believe me, Jack—it hasn't changed."

It was insane, agreeing to see Stephanie again. It was even more insane, not telling Jack the truth.

Talk about a breach of ethics… David's hands tightened on the steering wheel of his Porsche as he turned off the highway at the exit for Willingham Corners. He'd driven down instead of flying, telling himself that the hours on the road would clear his head.

Even a first-year law student would know that what he was doing was improper. He was the wrong man to deliver legal advice to the widow Willingham.

I already know her, he should have said to Jack. I've had a run-in with her.

A run-in? Hell, he'd almost ripped off her clothes.

It wasn't too late to turn back. To head for the nearest phone, call Jack, tell him…what?

Hello, Jack. Listen, I spent an afternoon trying to seduce the grieving widow, so I'll have to disqualify myself from this case.

But there was no case. He was only a messenger and if Stephanie had any faint hopes of going into a courtroom again, she'd change her mind once he'd laid out the facts.

David smiled thinly, and tromped down on the gas.

CHAPTER SIX

DUST rose into the air as Stephanie lugged her suitcase down from the shelf in the attic.

She sneezed, wiped her nose on the sleeve of her sweatshirt, and dumped the suitcase on the floor.

This was not the best place to spend an already warm May morning. The attic was airless and hot. Dust and cobwebs clung to every surface, spiders skittered in the corners and every now and then she caught the sound of mice behind the walls.

Stephanie shivered, despite the heat. She hoped they were mice, anyway.

The attic was depressing, too. It wasn't the kind of place that made you want to open old trunks and delve through the contents, despite the fact that it was a repository of cast-off furniture and knickknacks that dated back two centuries. Under ordinary circumstances, she'd probably have been fascinated by the stuff—but these weren't ordinary circumstances, and never had been.

"You have married into a fine old family," Clare had said on their wedding day, "but you will never be part of it."

Stephanie smiled grimly as she slammed the attic door behind her and edged her way down the steep wooden steps with her suitcase in her hand.

"I'll do my best to fit in," she'd said—but that was when she was still naive, when she'd believed in Avery's promises and in his kindness.

"Your best could never be good enough," Clare had replied with a brittle smile, and Stephanie, stung, had started to answer but Avery's hand had tightened painfully on hers and he'd drawn her into a corner. It had been the first indication of what her life as his wife was really going to be.

"Lesson one," he'd said with a phony smile plastered to his face so that anyone watching would think he was only whispering sweet nothings in her ear. "Don't you never sass my sister, you understand?"

Oh, yes, she'd understood. Avery had lied...but what could she do about it? He was all that stood between her and despair.

Stephanie carried the suitcase down the hall and into her bedroom. The lies, at least, were over now. She had no place to live, no money, and her brother's bills to meet, but at least she didn't have to pretend anymore. That was something to be grateful for, although she hadn't done much to keep up the pretense that she was glad to be Avery's wife the last couple of years. It hadn't been necessary. Avery had been too sick to appear in public very often. There'd been no reason to smile when he told a vulgar joke, or try not to shudder when he put his arm around her.

There'd been no reason to do much of anything—but she'd done it anyway, slept in the room next to his, as she'd done from the beginning; tended him when he woke during the night, gave him his medicines and fed him his meals and cleaned up his messes when he'd refused to let the nurses do it, because, after all, she'd given her word.

If only Avery had adhered to the same philosophy.

No. Stephanie opened the suitcase and stared down at the things inside it. She wouldn't think about that. She wouldn't think about anything, not until she spoke with Jack Russell's associate.

A woman from his office had phoned late yesterday. Mr. Russell was sending a colleague to meet with her, she'd said. Not Mr. Russell himself? Stephanie had asked, trying not to let her disappointment show. No, the woman had said briskly. An associate. A gentleman, who'd be paying a courtesy call in late afternoon.

After she hung up the phone, Stephanie realized she'd neglected to ask the gentleman's name. Not that it mattered. She was in no position to make demands on Mr. Russell. So long as he wasn't sending the office boy, she'd be satisfied. Russell's firm was well-respected. Avery had said as much once, in a left-handed way.

"Ol' Jack's the one man in Washington I've never been able to buy," he'd said with a wheezing laugh.

Stephanie blew a tangle of curls off her forehead. As far as she was concerned, there couldn't have been a better recommendation.

"Okay," she muttered, "let's see what's still usable here."

A musty smell wafted from the suitcase as she opened it. Stephanie wrinkled her nose, went to the windows and threw them open. Then she bent over the neatly folded clothing she'd put away seven long years ago…

And groaned.

The smell came from mildew, though that wasn't the worst of it. Something had gnawed a tiny hole in the corner of the lid, just big enough to have given the moths and mice a treat. Two dresses, both made on an ancient sewing machine, a pair of polyester slacks that could almost pass for wool, the blouses she'd put away with such care…all ruined.

"Burn that garbage," Avery had ordered the day she'd first come to this house.

The thought of tossing out what little remained of her old life, her real life, had terrified her. So, instead, she'd committed her first act of defiance and stashed the suitcase in the attic.

Stephanie sank down on the edge of the bed. It was silly, she knew, but she really had wanted to leave with nothing that wasn't her own. In view of the mess she'd found inside the suitcase, her choice was reduced to the jeans, sweatshirt and sneakers she was already wearing.

"Hell," she whispered, and shot to her feet.

It was even sillier, to sit here and waste time worrying about it.

"On to Plan Two, Steff," she said briskly.

She wiped her grimy hands on the seat of her jeans, then pulled open the closet door. Designer clothing crowded the rack from one wall to the other. Stephanie put out a hand, then drew it back.

"You're being an idiot," she muttered. "Clothing is clothing, that's all it is."

Exactly. And the cold truth was that she'd worked long and hard for her keep.

"Damn right," she said, and she began stripping garments from their hangers. Not too many—just enough until she found a job. Found a way to earn money for herself...

For Paul.

But how? How? She didn't need much to live on, but the costs of keeping her brother safe, and well, and reasonably content...

Why was she wasting time on a line of thought that wouldn't accomplish anything?

She worked quickly, folding things and placing them on the bed. Shoes, underwear, a sweater...

The sound of tires crunching on the bluestone gravel driveway drifted up through the opened windows.

Stephanie glanced at her watch and frowned. Who could that be? It was early afternoon; Russell's man wasn't due until much later and she wasn't expecting anyone else...

Clare.

Of course. It would be her sister-in-law, come to gloat, to remind her that she had to be out of here by midnight.

The doorbell rang. Stephanie shot a look into the mirror. She was a mess. She had no makeup on, her hair seemed to have forgotten its morning touch of the comb. Her sweatshirt was grimy, her jeans were torn and she'd snagged a couple of fingernails wrestling the suitcase from the attic.

She looked like hell—and hell was exactly what Clare deserved.

She took a deep breath and headed for the stairs.

David stood on the porch, his hands tucked into the back pockets of his chinos, whistling softly through his teeth as he surveyed the scene around him.

Big white house, colonnaded porch, a driveway you damn near needed a map to negotiate and enough Spanish moss dripping from the trees to gladden the heart of the entire Confederate army.

Nice. Very nice—assuming that living on the set of *Gone with the Wind* was your idea of a good time. It sure as hell wasn't his and somehow, he wouldn't have thought it suited the widow Willingham, either, but then, what he knew about the woman could fit in a thimble with room left to spare.

Frowning, he jabbed the doorbell again. Wouldn't it be a bitch if she wasn't in? He knew he was early, knew he probably should have phoned from his car, but there'd been no way to precisely estimate his arrival time...

Who was he kidding? He hadn't phoned because he was damned well certain Stephanie would have told him what he could do with his impending visit, had she known about it. And then she'd have seen to it that Jack knew the details, as well. All the details, including the embarrassing ones. So David had instructed his temp to offer no names to Mrs. Willingham.

"Just tell her to expect a visit from a member of Mr. Russell's firm," he'd said.

The woman's brows had taken a barely perceptible lift but, unlike the late, unlamented Miss Murchison, she hadn't asked any questions.

"Yes, sir," she'd replied, and now here he was, unembarrassed...and, thanks to the hour, unexpected.

David stepped off the porch and gave the house the once-over again. Windows were open upstairs; he could see draperies billowing gently under the warm caress of the spring breeze. Okay. One last try. He climbed the steps, crossed the porch, and pressed the bell, listening as the chimes echoed distantly through the rooms.

All right. Enough was enough. He'd head back to the highway. Or to his car. Yes, that's what he'd do, phone Jack and tell him what he should have told him in the first place, that he was the wrong man to deal with the beautiful young widow with the vulnerable air and the disposition of a tigress...

The door swung open. Stephanie Willingham stood before him, her hands on her hips.

"You know what, Clare?" she was saying. "As far as I'm concerned, you can take this miserable house and—"

She broke off, her face reflecting shock. Not that David really noticed. He was pretty much in shock, himself.

This wasn't the stunning, sophisticated woman he'd been dreaming about . Stephanie looked about as sophisticated as a teenager. And she was—there was no other word to describe her—a mess. Her face was smudged and makeup-free; her hair was a mass of ringlets. She was wearing a sweatshirt that was a couple of sizes too large and a pair of jeans that had definitely seen better days.

And she was definitely not as beautiful as he'd remembered.

She was more beautiful, so lovely that the shock of seeing her almost stole his breath.

As it was, it damn near stole his hand, which he'd rested on the doorjamb.

"You," Stephanie said, and slammed the door in his face.

He moved fast, got his hand out of the way just in time and replaced it with his shoulder, wincing when the door threatened its removal.

"Okay," he said, "calm down."

"How dare you? How *dare* you?"

"Mrs. Willingham...Stephanie..."

She called him a name, one that made his eyes widen.

"Get out of here! You hear me? You—get—out—of—here—right—now," she said, punctuating each word with a shove against the door.

"Hey. Hey, don't do that. You're going to slice my arm off at the shoulder."

"That'll be a good start, you—you..."

"Look, I know you're not glad to see me, but—"

"Not glad? *Not glad?*" Her voice flew up the scales. "Get off my porch. Get out of my driveway. Get—"

"Dammit, woman, listen to me!"

"No, Mr. Chambers. You're the one has to do the listening." Her eyes narrowed coldly. "I've got a shotgun right at my side."

"Oh, for crying out loud..."

"My late husband always said a loaded gun was a man's best friend, but believe me, this gun's got nothing against being a woman's best friend, too."

"Listen, there's a perfectly logical explanation for—"

''You get yourself out of this doorway, down those steps and into your car or so help me Hannah, I'll blow your head off!''

Did she really have a gun? David hadn't seen any, but what did that prove? Not seeing a weapon didn't mean there wasn't a weapon. That was urban survival lesson number one.

''Mrs. Willingham,'' he said in his finest, most conciliatory-courtroom manner, ''you're overreacting.''

''Move, Mr. Chambers!''

''Stephanie, dammit because—''

''One-one thousand. Two-one thousand. Three-one thou—''

''What are you doing?''

''I'm counting. You have five seconds, sir. Two more, in other words, and if I'm not looking at your backside by then, I'm going to fire.''

David sighed. ''Jack Russell,'' he said, and the instant he saw her eyebrows knot together in puzzlement, he twisted hard, freed his shoulder and threw all his weight against the door.

She had the advantage of leverage. He, however, he had a multiplicity of advantages. He had weight. Height. Muscle. And the growing conviction that if she really did have a gun, she wouldn't hesitate to use it.

The wood groaned. Stephanie shrieked. And then the door gave and he barreled through the opening and damn near through her, too. She shrieked again as his momentum carried him forward, onto her. Together, they fell against the wall.

David's elbow hit first. Dimly, in the back of his mind, he was aware of a lancet of pain and the knowledge that his arm would probably hurt like hell later on.

Mostly, he was aware of her.

Of Stephanie. Her softness, and the fullness of her breasts, braless apparently, beneath the oversize sweatshirt. Of the silky brush of her hair against his mouth. The faint, incredibly sexy aroma of woman and flowers and sweat...

And of her knee, as she aimed it straight for the most vulnerable part of his anatomy.

David cursed and sidestepped just in time. She caught him in the thigh instead of where she'd been aiming, but it was close enough so that he got the message.

There was no gun—his brain had registered that fact right away—but that didn't mean she wasn't hell-bent on murder.

''Okay,'' he said grimly as she struggled to get a thumb in his eye and a knee to his groin. His hands closed on her wrists; he lifted her arms and pinned them to the wall above her head. "Okay, Scarlett, that's enough!"

"I'll scream," she panted. "And everybody in this house will come running. The maid. The butler. The chauffeur. The cook. The housekeeper…"

"Funny not a one of them came running when I was leaning on that doorbell," David said with a mirthless smile, "or when you were screaming up a storm, a couple of minutes ago."

Color drained from her face. "They're— they're all busy."

"Busy." He smiled silkily. "Of course. Why didn't I think of that? No well-trained servant would interrupt his or her work to respond to a doorbell or, heaven forbid, a woman's bloodcurdling screams."

"They're all here, I'm telling you."

"Sure they are."

"I've only to call them—"

"Call."

"—And they'll come running."

"Tripping over each other's feet, as they rush to your aid, right?"

"Yes. No. I mean—"

"I know what you mean, Scarlett. I'm just not buying. You've told one tall tale too many. First a loaded rifle—"

"A shotgun," Stephanie said with surprising dignity.

"And now a bunch of stalwart servants near at hand." David grinned. "You've certainly got a fine imagination."

Color seeped back into her face, along the elegant, high arches of her cheeks.

"And you've got your nerve, coming here!"

"I've been trying to tell you, I'm here for a reason…and not the one you think."

But he was having increasing trouble, remembering the reason for his visit. The supposed reason because, the truth was, he'd been searching for an excuse to find this woman ever since he'd turned his back on her in that airplane and walked away.

He could see the swiftness of her pulse beating in the hollow of her throat. She wasn't frightened of him anymore; the magic words—Jack Russell—had taken care of that. She was just wary now, and angry.

And so damn gorgeous.

She was breathing rapidly, and not even the fullness of the sweatshirt could disguise the rise and fall of her rounded breasts. He was still holding her hands locked above her head; the position of her arms tilted her body forward ever so slightly and his weight was still on her—it had been the only way to keep that knee from getting him where he lived—and now, for the first time, he registered the fact that her hips were angled toward his, that her pelvis was tight against him.

Heat rose in his loins and raced through his blood; he saw her pupils enlarge as she felt the immediacy of his arousal against her. The pulse in her throat beat faster, and his heart raced along with it. She knew what was happening, and she was responding to it. She wanted him, wanted what he knew now he had never stopped wanting.

He slid his hands up her throat, to her face. Her skin felt cool against his fingertips. His thumb slid across her mouth, and her lips parted.

God, he was on fire!

He whispered her name, his voice husky and thick with need. The sound of it seemed to startle her. He felt her stiffen against him, and saw the sudden contraction of her pupils.

''Don't,'' she said. ''Please, don't.'' And even in the escalating fever of his desire, David recognized the fear in that soft, breathless plea.

It stunned him.

He'd known many women over the years. Some had claimed to adore him, one—his former wife—to despise him, but none had ever feared him. It was a new experience, and an ugly one.

There was nothing lower than a man who inspired fear in women.

And Stephanie wasn't just afraid. She was terrified.

His hands slid to her shoulders. He felt her start to tremble.

"Listen to me. I'm not going to hurt you. I'd never hurt you—"

"Let go of me!"

He did, immediately, although what he really wanted to do was take her into his arms, hold her close, promise her that no one would ever hurt her, not so long as he was there...

"Now, get out of my house." She pointed her finger at the door. Her hand was shaking, but her voice was clear and steady.

"Jack Russell asked me to talk to you."

"I don't believe you!"

"Jack told me you'd phoned him about a legal problem. He asked me if I'd come down and discuss it with you."

Her eyes narrowed. "Why would he do that? And how do you know Mr. Russell?"

"He and I are partners in the same law firm. He told me you needed legal advice."

She stared at him, speechless, and then she gave a choked laugh.

"Let me get this straight. You're his errand boy?"

David's mouth thinned. "I'm no one's errand boy. Jack asked me to talk to you and I said I would, as a favor. To Jack," he added with deliberate emphasis.

Was he telling her the truth? she wondered. Probably. He couldn't have found out about her call to Russell any other way. Not that it changed the facts. Given the choice between finding Godzilla and David Chambers on her doorstep, she'd have opted for the reptile, and never mind that it wasn't the one who had the law degree.

Stephanie stood as straight and tall as her five feet, four inches permitted.

"Well, you've done it. You've come here to see me—and now you can go home." Her chin tilted. "You can inform Mr. Russell that you did as he'd requested, and that I sent you packing."

"No loss, Scarlett. I always thought this was a complete waste of time. I told Jack straight off that you haven't got a case."

"Thank you for your opinion, Mr. Chambers. And goodbye."

"I'll give Jack your regards."

"You do that."

He nodded, stepped out onto the porch, started toward the steps... Hell, he thought angrily, and swung toward her.

"I was wrong."

"Indeed you were."

"It *is* a loss. Mine—considering that I've already wasted the day."

"What a pity," she said sweetly.

"Yeah. I'm sure it breaks your heart that I expected to be back home on my ranch just about now."

"My goodness," she purred. "I didn't know they had ranches up there in the nation's capitol." And she laughed softly in a way that made him want to walk over, grab her and shake her until she stopped laughing...

Or grab her and kiss her until she melted in his arms.

A muscle knotted in David's cheek.

"It seems to me you've got a choice here," he said, his tone brusque. "You can feel smug about knowing my weekend's shot to hell, thanks to you, or you can come down off that high horse and tell me your story." David swept back his tweed jacket and slapped his hands onto his hips. "Your choice, though frankly, I don't give a damn what you decide."

He didn't, either; Stephanie could see it in his stance. And in his face. That hard, handsome face that she'd thought of so many times during the past days and nights, although why she should have was beyond her.

Everything about him was exactly as she'd remembered. His hair was drawn back in that sexy ponytail; his skin had that golden tanned look that nobody had ever gotten from a bottle or a sunlamp. The well-tailored dark suit, snowy-white shirt and silk tie of two weeks ago had given way to a gray tweed jacket, a pale blue cotton sweater and a pair of chino trousers. His boots were dark brown this time, and scuffed just enough so they looked as if they'd seen real use. Not that they would have. She could just imagine his ranch, with yards of manicured lawn and hot-and-cold running servants, and a big, paneled den lined with the heads of dead animals where he sat pretending to be a Western Hero while outside, other men sweated and worked their butts off on his behalf...

"—Your mind."

Stephanie blinked. "I didn't...what did you say?"

"I said..." He glanced purposefully at his watch. "Make up your mind. If I'm going to be heading back to Washington, I'd just as soon get started.'' He smiled coolly. "Maybe I can get back in time to do something pleasant with my Friday night.''

Call some woman, he meant. Take her someplace cozy for dinner, then bring her back to his place, take her in his arms...

Which was none of her business. Absolutely none.

"Well?'' he demanded. ''What's it going to be?''

Not that he needed to ask. David almost smiled. Stephanie's face was like an open book. She wanted to tell him to go. Maybe it was more accurate to say that what she really wanted was to push him down the steps and off the porch.

But she also wanted him to stay. That didn't surprise him. She'd called Jack for help; to turn that help away now would be stupid, and whatever else she was, the widow Willingham was not dumb.

He shot back his sleeve, looked at his watch again, and that did it.

"You're right,'' she said, the words rushed together as if she knew that if she didn't say them quickly, she'd never manage to say them at all. "I suppose I've no choice in the matter.''

"There's always a choice, Scarlett. I'm sure you've been around long enough to know that.''

She smiled bitterly at the thinly veiled condemnation in his voice. How smug he was. How sure of himself. How totally, completely, thoughtlessly male.

She thought of telling him so, of adding that if he really believed there were always choices, he'd either been born with a silver spoon in his mouth or with an IQ rivaling that of a slug.

Stephanie turned on her heel and strode toward an arched doorway at the end of the enormous hall. "Very well, Mr. Chambers. I'll give you ten minutes."

"No."

Incredulous, she spun toward him. "No? But you just said—"

"*You* are not giving me anything," David said in a clipped tone. "Let's be sure we understand that from the start." He eyed her stonily. "I'm the one who's giving *you* something. And if you can't get that straight, I'm out of here."

Her face bloomed with color. "I do not like you, Mr. Chambers," she said. "Let us be sure *you* understand that!"

He laughed. "Why, Scarlett, darlin', you just about break mah heart."

"I'd take that as a compliment—except we both know you haven't got a heart." Stephanie jerked her head toward the doorway. "We can talk here, in the parlor."

David hesitated. *Step into my parlor, said the spider to the fly...*

"Are you coming, sir? Or have you suddenly changed your mind?"

Change it, David told himself. *Don't be an idiot, Chambers.*

"Don't be silly," he said with a tight smile. "I wouldn't miss our little talk for anything."

And he sauntered down the hall and stepped past her, into the parlor.

CHAPTER SEVEN

THE room suited the house, or perhaps it suited David's expectations.

It was big and overdone, a relic of a bygone era. And it was meant to impress, assuming you were the sort who'd be impressed by dark velvet sofas and chairs that looked as if they'd buckle under a person's weight. Lamps topped with fringed silk shades fought for space on tables crowded with an army of gilt cupids and porcelain shepherdesses.

"Sit down, Mr. Chambers." Stephanie yanked open the top drawer of a mahogany rolltop desk. "That green love seat's probably the most comfortable spot, and you can turn on the lamp beside it."

David looked at the love seat in question. "Comfortable" was not a word he'd have used to describe it, but then, compared to the other chairs and sofas in the cavernous room, he figured she might have been right. He ran his hand over the rectangle of white lace centered on the headrest.

"Antimacassars," he said with a little laugh. "I didn't think they made them anymore."

Stephanie turned toward him, a sheaf of papers in her hand. Something that resembled a smile pulled at the corners of her lips. "*They* don't, but Clare does."

"Your sister-in-law?"

"Correct. Antimacassars aren't popular items in today's world. I'm surprised you'd even know the word."

"I had an aunt who had antimacassars draped over every chair and sofa in what she called 'the front room.'" David strolled to a fireplace that looked big enough to house a family of four, tucked his hands into the back pockets of his chinos and put one booted foot up on the hearth. "The room was off-limits, but sometimes, when we were visiting, I used to sneak inside. It was kind of like stepping into a time warp. Chairs that creaked when you sat down, lampshades hung with dusty..." He frowned, as if he'd just realized what he was saying, and cleared his throat. "Not that this is anything like Aunt Min's front room," he said quickly. "This is, well, it's...interesting."

"Don't try and be polite, Mr. Chambers. It would be too out of character. Besides, there's no need to mince words. This room is not interesting. It's ugly. Everybody knew it, except for my husband.'' She tapped the stack of papers on the edge of the desk, squared off the edges and handed them to him. ''This is all the correspondence I've had with my lawyer, with the judge, with Dawes and Smith…''

''Clare's attorneys?''

''That's right.''

David fanned through the documents. ''Impressive.''

''But meaningless. I'd lost the battle before the first shot was fired.''

''Yes. Jack told me your husband and his sister held all his property jointly. That means—''

''I know what it means,'' Stephanie said impatiently. ''I also know what Avery promised me—''

''Money,'' David said.

''The money I'm entitled to.'' Her face pinkened but her head was high. ''As for what I meant about losing the battle before the first shot was fired…you should be aware that there isn't a person in this county who wanted me to collect a dime from my late husband's estate.''

''What people want has little to do with what the law determines.''

Stephanie laughed. ''Mr. Chambers, look around you. You're standing in Avery Willingham's home, in the town named for his great-great-great-grandfather. Maybe I left out a great or two—I never did get it straight. My husband owned this town and the people in it. Everyone admired him and revered him—''

''Everyone,'' David said, his eyes on her face, ''except for you.''

Stephanie's gaze never wavered. ''Have you come here to pass judgment, sir, or to tender advice? If it's judgment, I've had enough to last a lifetime and you can just turn around and go straight out the door. If it's advice, I suggest you read through those papers and then tell me what you think.''

David smiled. ''I gather you're not an advocate for delicate Southern womanhood, Mrs. Willingham.''

''Delicacy is an indulgence,'' Stephanie said coolly, folding her arms, ''and I have neither the time nor the patience for it.''

''No.'' His tone was the chilly equal of hers. ''Not with your husband's assets at stake.''

She didn't so much as blink. ''That's right. So, what's it going to be? Are you going to read those documents or are you going to leave?''

Amazing, he thought. This woman only gave the appearance of fragility. Under that delicate exterior, she had a strength he admired, even if he didn't admire the greed that drove it.

"Well? What's it going to be, Mr. Chambers?"

Logic and reason told him that his best bet would be to dump the papers on the nearest table, but he'd put in long hours on the road to get here. What would be the point in walking out now? Besides, he was doing this for Jack, not for the widow Willingham. So he walked to the love seat she'd designated as comfortable, undid the buttons on his jacket and cautiously eased his six-foot-two-inch frame onto the bottle green velvet.

"Brew me a pot of strong coffee and give me an hour," he said, "and then we'll talk."

Stephanie fought to keep the relief from showing on her face. For a minute or two, she'd thought David might really drop her papers into her arms and march out the door. And she hadn't wanted that, despite her threats. She needed his advice...and needing his advice was surely the sole reason she'd want anything whatsoever to do with this man.

She watched as he began reading the first page. After a minute, he frowned, half rose, shrugged off his jacket and tossed it aside. Then he sat back and pushed up the sleeves of his cotton sweater, all the while never taking his eyes from the page.

He'd already forgotten her presence. Well, she was accustomed to that. Avery used to do the same thing... No. It wasn't the same. Her husband had deliberately ignored her. It had been a way of showing her her proper place in his life, but David was oblivious to her because he'd lost himself in reading the documents. His brow was furrowed in concentration, and those piercingly blue eyes were fixed on the printed page.

Her gaze fell to his hands. They were powerful, and very masculine. His forearms were muscular and lightly dusted with dark hair. He should have looked as out of place as a weight lifter at a tea party, perched on the ridiculous love seat with his boots planted firmly on the flowered rug, but he didn't. He looked—he looked big, and wonderfully rugged, and he dominated the room with his presence.

"Do I get that coffee or not?"

She started at the brusqueness of his voice. He looked up, his expression unreadable, and then he gave her a smile that could only be described as patronizing.

"Or is making coffee a skill you haven't mastered?"

"You'd be shocked at the skills I've mastered," Stephanie said with frigid disdain.

No, David thought as she swept from the room, hell, no, he wouldn't...and then he took a deep breath, forced his mind back from where it was threatening to wander, and focused on the law.

The law, at least, always made sense.

He was barely aware of Stephanie placing a silver serving tray on the table beside him. He reached out, located the cup of coffee by feel, and took a sip. It was black, hot and strong, and surpassingly good. He acknowledged it with a curt nod.

The next time he surfaced, the cup, and the pot, were both empty. Stephanie was sitting across from him, her feet crossed at the ankles, her hands folded tightly in her lap.

"You drank it all," she said. "Do you want me to make more?"

David shook his head, rotated his shoulders, and lifted the papers from the cushion beside him.

"No, that's fine. I'm done reading." He rose and walked to the secretary.

"And?" Stephanie said. "What do you think?"

He swung around and faced her. He could see her fingers knotting together. She was apprehensive, and he could hardly blame her. She'd invested half a dozen years, maybe more, in a project named Avery Willingham, and now she was about to be cut out of the payoff.

"And," he said with a smile as bright as a shark's, "your chances of changing the judge's decision range from slim to none."

"I don't want to change his decision. I thought you understood that. Clare can have everything. I only want what I'm entitled to."

"Nothing. That's what you're entitled to, in the eyes of the law."

Stephanie nodded. Her face gave nothing away. "Well, then, I guess that's—"

"There was no pretense about it, I have to give you that much," David said, his voice harsh.

"No pretense?"

"About why you decided to snag Willingham." He jerked his head toward the secretary, and the documents. "It was a tradeoff, plain and simple. He put money in the piggy bank, and you gave him what he wanted. I have to hand it to you, Scarlett. You look like a throwback to Jane Austen, but the truth is that you've got a cash register where most people have a heart."

Stephanie flushed and rose to her feet. "Contrary to the sleazy little script you've worked up, Mr. Chambers, I did not set out to *snag* Avery. I knew him for many years. I worked for him, as his secretary." David snorted and she stalked toward him, eyes flashing with anger. "I was a damn good secretary, too!"

"Until you looked around and saw that there was a chance at a better-paying job."

"You're like all the rest. You know it all, and don't give a damn for the truth!"

"Tell it to me, then," David said, his laughter suddenly gone. "Give me something to go on, something that makes this look like anything but what it is."

"Prove my innocence, you mean? I thought lawyers were supposed to defend their clients, regardless of guilt or innocence."

"You've got your facts twisted, Scarlett. You're not my client, remember? As for guilt or innocence...there's none at issue here."

"Then why do you expect me to defend myself to you?"

"I don't."

"Good. Because I don't intend to." Stephanie slapped her hands on her hips. "But I'll tell you this much. I was Avery's secretary for a year. And then..." Her throat constricted as she swallowed. "And then he said what he really needed was a wife. Someone to run his home and entertain his guests."

David's smile was wolfish. "And I'll bet you were even better at providing entertainment than you were at taking dictation."

"In return," she said, refusing to be drawn into the game, "Avery agreed to—to compensate me.

It was his idea, all of it. The marriage, the terms…and the money.''

''And you jumped at the offer.''

Stephanie thought of the shock she'd felt when Avery had proposed the arrangement, of how she'd agonized over it; of how he had reassured her that it was the only way she could ensure proper care for Paul…

And of his promise that nothing between them would change.

''Is this how the law is practiced on your turf, Mr. Chambers?'' Her voice was cool and steady. It had to be. She would show no weakness, ever again. ''Do lawyers get to be judge and jury, too?''

He smiled in a way that made her want to take a step back.

''No. They don't.'' He began moving toward her and she couldn't help it, she did take a step back, then another, until her shoulders hit the wall. ''Frankly, I've always thought that was unfortunate. After a while, most lawyers can pretty much tell if a client's telling them the truth—or a load of bull.''

''I'm not your client, remember?''

''It's a good story, Scarlett, and you tell it well. But the simple truth is that you conned Avery Willingham into marriage. Well, maybe that's a bit harsh.'' His smile sent shivers up her spine. ''What you did was set out the bait. Then you settled back, waited—''

''Get out of my house!''

''What's the problem? Is the truth too rough for your delicate tastes?'' Darkness filled his eyes. ''Or is there another truth, one that I've somehow missed? If there is, tell it to me now.''

Of course, there was another truth. The *only* truth. But she had made a promise to Paul, one she would not break.

''The late Mr. Willingham bought you.'' His voice was flat and harsh. ''Twenty-five hundred bucks a month, deposited into an account in your name. That was the deal.''

''Yes,'' she said. ''That was the deal.''

David nodded calmly, even though he felt as if someone had punched him in the gut. He looked down into those chocolate eyes. What had he expected? That she'd weep? That she'd spill some incredible tale explaining that she'd been forced into the marriage? He'd come to this house, knowing the truth. She'd sold herself to the highest bidder. She'd gone to a man's bed for money...

But it was desire that would have brought her to his bed, had he asked. She'd moaned with need in his arms, returned his kisses with a passion he still remembered, and he hadn't bought those moments with coins dropped into a till. He could make her moan again, want him again, even now. All he had to do was reach out for her...

David cursed under his breath. He strode past her, took a couple of deep breaths, just enough to be sure he had himself under control again, then turned around.

"You wanted my legal advice, and here it is." His eyes met hers. "Remember that old saw about shutting the barn door after the horse is gone?"

"Meaning?"

"Meaning, it's too late. You should have consulted a lawyer before you agreed to marry Willingham."

"Avery was a lawyer," she said softly. "He assured me that he'd take care of everything."

"Yeah, well, he certainly did. He fixed it so the gravy train stopped the day he died."

"I thought—I hoped my—my arrangement with my husband could be construed as a kind of contract," Stephanie said softly.

"You mean, an oral contract?" David shook his head. "You'd need a disinterested witness, or at least a set of circumstances that would make a reasonable person think such a contract might have been possible. Your best hope would be to find a judge who'd take pity on you and agree that a man couldn't cut his wife off without a dime...but you've already traveled that route.''

She nodded, put her hands into the pockets of her jeans and looked down at the floor. For the very first time, there was the slump of defeat in her shoulders. Despite what he knew about her, David felt a twinge of sympathy.

''Do you think Mr. Russell would agree with your opinion?''

''Yes,'' he said, because there was no point in lying.

''Well.'' She swallowed, lifted her head, and looked him squarely in the eye. ''Thank you for your trouble, Mr. Chambers.''

''You could contact another attorney, not the one who represented you before, ask if he'd take the case on.''

''No. You've made it very clear that it would be an impossible battle, and besides, no one around here would touch this.'' She held out her hand. ''Again, I thank you for your trouble—''

''I suppose,'' David said, ''I could get you a stay, so that you wouldn't have to vacate the house by today.''

She drew back her hand, tucked it into her pocket, and shook her head. ''There's no sense in delaying the inevitable.''

"Do you have a place to go?"

"Of course," she said instantly, the lie tripping from her tongue with amazing ease, but there wasn't a way in the world she was going to let anyone—David, especially—know how bad her situation was.

"And you have something stashed away to live on." His smile was quick and unpleasant. "All that money, going into your account month after month... It must have piled up a tidy bit of interest by now."

Lying the second time was even easier. "Certainly," she said briskly. She brushed by him and made her way toward the hall. "Thank you for your time, and please thank Mr. Russell, too. Now, if you don't mind, I have a great deal to do—"

"I just keep wondering," David said, "did you give your husband value for his money?"

She swung toward him, her face drained of color. "That's none of your business!"

"Actually, it is."

What in the name of heaven are you doing, Chambers? a voice inside him whispered in amazement, but he ignored it. The grim truth was, he'd passed the point of no return two weeks ago, on the plane to Washington.

"It's very much my business," he said. "As your attorney—"

"One of us is crazy, Mr. Chambers. You've just gone out of your way to make it clear that you are *not* my attorney."

"Semantics," he said, mixing first-year law with any-year gibberish. "I've given you legal counsel, haven't I?"

"You have, yes, but—"

"Then, I'd be negligent if I didn't ask if you'd kept your part of what you say may have been an oral contract."

"But you just said—"

"I know what I said." He didn't. He didn't even know what he was saying now. He only knew that he had to touch her again, that something was stretching and stirring deep within a hidden, primitive part of him. She looked so lost, so alone. "I need more information," he said reasonably, as he walked toward her, stopping when they were inches apart. "About your relationship with Willingham."

He looked down into Stephanie's puzzled, upturned face. At the dark eyes that could shine with an innocence he knew to be a sham, then cloud over with desire in a heartbeat. He reached out and ran the back of his hand along her cheek. She jerked away, like a skittish colt.

"Did he please you?" he said gruffly. "Aside from the money, I mean. Were you happy with him?"

"You've no right to ask me such—"

"Did you tremble when he touched you?"

He put his hand against the curve of her cheek, dropped it to her throat. His fingers were hot against her skin and she caught her breath, stiffening herself against his touch, trying to deny what it made her feel because it was impossible. She couldn't—she mustn't...

"You trembled when I touched you," he said, his voice low and rough. "Just as you are now."

"Stop," she said, but her voice was a thready whisper. "David, stop."

His gaze dropped to her mouth. Her lips parted, as he'd known they would. He felt the rush of heat racing through his body, felt the tension spreading until his nerve endings seemed to hum. He said her name, drew her into his arms, thrust his hands into her hair and tangled his fingers in its sensuous weight.

"David," she whispered, and her breath caught. "David?"

"Yes," he said, drowning in what he saw in her eyes. "That's right. David. Only David..."

He kissed her. Or she kissed him. In the end, it didn't matter. The fusion was complete.

Mouths, bodies... Where did she begin and he end? He didn't know, didn't care, didn't want to think about it because nothing else mattered but the feel of Stephanie, warm and willing, in his arms.

CHAPTER EIGHT

NOTHING mattered, but being in David's arms.

Stephanie felt weightless, as she melted into him. All rational thought was gone.

The feel of him. The warmth of his body. The touch of his hot, hungry mouth on hers. She was spinning, spinning, like a planet around an incandescent sun.

She heard him whisper her name as he slid his hands up her body, cupped her face and held her willingly captive to his kiss. He said something against her mouth. She couldn't understand the words but she knew what he must be asking, and her answer was in the way she touched him and moved against him.

"Scarlett." His voice was urgent as he cupped her bottom, lifted her into the heat and hardness of his arousal, urged her to feel the raw, masculine power she had unleashed.

The reality should have terrified her, as it had in the past. But what she felt was excitement. This was—David was—every half-forgotten dream of her girlhood. He was a million unfulfilled wishes, and more.

"Tell me what you want," he said. He cupped her breast, pressed his mouth to her throat. "Say that it's me, Scarlett. Say—"

"Well, heavens to Betsy! Now, isn't this a charmin' sight?"

They sprang apart. Instinctively, David put Stephanie behind him as they turned toward the hall.

He saw a woman in the arched doorway. His lawyer's mind made a fast inventory. She was, perhaps, two decades older than Stephanie with a heavily made-up face, a mane of frizzy hair whose platinum color could only have come from a bottle, and eyes a shade of green that had to have started life on an optician's workbench. She was poured into a leopard-print cat suit that was at least a size too small. And a cat, David thought, was what she looked like, one that had just opened its mouth and swallowed a live canary.

Stephanie stepped out from behind him. "Clare?"

Avery Willingham's sister. David's eyes narrowed.

"In the flesh," Clare said. Smiling, she strolled toward them, breasts jiggling under the clinging cat suit. "And who, pray tell, is your charmin' visitor?"

Stephanie moved forward, and the women met in the center of the room. Her mouth still bore the faint swelling that was the imprint of his kisses, her cheeks were still flushed, but somehow she'd managed to take on an aura of composure and command. Even to his jaundiced eye, it was a remarkable performance.

"What are you doing here, Clare?"

Clare smiled. "What am I doin' here? she asks. This is my house, missy. I don't need a reason to be in it."

"It isn't yours, not until midnight."

Clare shrugged. "A technicality."

"Until then," Stephanie said calmly, "please ring the doorbell if you wish to come in."

"I did, missy." Clare batted her heavily mascared lashes at David. "But there was no answer. 'Course, I understand the reason. You were… busy. You and Mister…"

"Chambers," David said. "David Chambers."

"A pleasure, Mr. Chambers. I'm awfully sorry if I interrupted anythin', but I had no idea Stephanie would be entertainin' a gentleman, this bein' such a busy weekend for her an' all."

David put his hand lightly on Stephanie's shoulder. Her posture was rigid but she was trembling; he could feel it through his fingertips.

''What do you want, Clare?'' she said.

''Why, just to make sure things are as they should be.'' The blonde gave David a last slow smile, then began circling the room, brushing long, fuchsia-lacquered fingernails over the gilt cherubs and porcelain shepherdesses. ''All of this is mine now, missy, these precious heirlooms that've been passed from one generation of Willin'hams to another. You just remember that.''

''How could I forget?''

''You're to take nothin', you understand that? Not a single thing.''

''You've nothing to worry about, Clare. I don't want any of this—this stuff. I intend to leave with nothing but the same suitcase I brought here.''

''Just you make sure there's nothin' in that suitcase but the junk you brought to this fine house, missy, you got that?''

Stephanie stepped out from under David's hand. She wasn't shaking anymore; he was sure of it.

''Your attorney already did an inventory,'' she said.

''An' how do I know that would stop you from takin' my things?'' Clare's eyes looked like bright green beads. "Trash like you is capable of anythin'."

"Go home, Clare." Stephanie's voice was low but firm. "You can do all the gloating you want, come midnight."

"And that big bedroom closet of yours, the one my brother kept filled. All that stuff's mine now. You just be sure an'—"

"The clothing is Mrs. Willingham's."

Both women looked at David. "I beg your pardon?" Clare said.

"I'm Mrs. Willingham's attorney, and I said the clothing belongs to her. It's her personal property."

Clare laughed. "Still not givin' up, are you, missy? Well, you're too late, Mister Attorney. The case has been settled."

"Whether it has or has not, Mrs. Willingham has certain rights. I've come here to make sure she is able to exercise them without interference."

Clare tossed back her peroxide mane. "Really. An' here I could have sworn you and my beloved sister-in-law were…well, I won't use the word. I'm too much a lady."

"Is that right?" David smiled lazily. "I'd have thought a lady would have known that breaking into a house was against the law."

"Don't be ridiculous! Seven Oaks belongs to me."

"Not until midnight."

"I have a key!"

David's brows rose. "Did you give this woman a key, Mrs. Willingham?"

Stephanie stared at him in amazement. In all these months, this was the first time anyone had ever come to her defense. Even Amos Turner, whom she'd paid for his legal services, had never said a word on her behalf except in judge's chambers.

Stephanie swallowed dryly. "No," she said. "No, I—"

"My client says she did not give you a key," David said pleasantly, "and I can attest to the fact that you neither asked permission to enter nor received it. Where I come from, that makes you an intruder until the time the court order takes effect."

Clare shot a baleful look at Stephanie. "You better tell this hotshot lawyer of yours that he's bein' stupid! Maybe he doesn't understand who I am!"

"He knows who you are," Stephanie said calmly. "And I suspect he knows what you are, too."

Clare's plump face took on a purplish tinge.

''I don't know what game you two think you're playin','' she snapped, ''but it isn't goin' to change one little thing. I'm tellin' you right here an' now, Miss High an' Mighty, you'd best be out of here by tonight.''

''With pleasure.''

''I heard about that call you made to the judge—''

''There's no need to go into details,'' Stephanie said quickly.

''Cryin' about needin' time to find a place to live and a job, moanin' about not havin' any money—''

''I said I don't want to discuss this now, Clare.''

''You came to Seven Oaks with nothin', and you're gonna leave with nothin'. You can sleep on the street, for all I care!''

''Is it true?'' David said quietly, his eyes locked on Stephanie's.

''It's none of your affair.''

''Stephanie, answer me! Do you have money, and a place to live?''

''She has nothin','' Clare said with ill-concealed glee. ''Nothin' a-tall!''

''Dammit,'' David growled, ''tell her she's wrong!''

Stephanie glared at him. "I can't, David. She's right. Now, are you satisfied?"

David's eyes narrowed. What in hell had she done with all the money Willingham had paid her? Not that it mattered to him. He'd come to her rescue a minute ago because it was the proper thing to do. No decent lawyer would stand by and let her give up property that was rightfully hers. But the rest of it, what happened to her after this...she was correct. It was none of his affair.

"Just you make sure there's nothin' of mine accidentally falls into your suitcase, when you leave my house."

"I wouldn't take anything from this house, Clare. I don't *want* anything that belonged to the Willinghams. Haven't you got that straight yet?"

"What *you'd* best get straight, missy, is that I expect everythin' I deserve. You hear?"

Stephanie looked at Clare, at the pudgy, selfish face and the piggy eyes. She'd had years of looking at that face, of listening to that whining voice.

"I hear," she said...and then, with a graceful movement of her hand that could almost have been accidental, she swept a tabletop's worth of ugly cupids and shepherdesses crashing to the floor.

No one moved. No one even breathed. Clare, Stephanie and David all looked down at the floor.

Stephanie was the first to raise her head.

"Oh, my," she said sweetly, "just look at what I've done. I don't know how I could have been so clumsy."

Clare, as puffed as a chicken ruffling its feathers, took a step forward. "Why, you—you—"

"Accidents will happen," David said, trying not to laugh. He looked at Stephanie, whose eyes were bright with defiance, and he felt a strange lurch inside his chest. "Isn't that right, Mrs. Willingham?"

"That's a fact," she said pleasantly.

"Accident?" Clare glared at them both. "That was no accident. She did it on purpose!"

"So sue her." David's smile held all the warmth of an iceberg.

"What for, wise guy? Your precious client is broke, or have you forgotten that?"

A muscle knotted in David's cheek. "No," he said quietly, "I haven't forgotten. Send the bills to me."

"David," Stephanie said, "this isn't necessary."

"It surely is!" Clare snatched David's business card from his outstretched hand. "The cost of replacin' these things will be horrendous. They're—"

"Priceless heirlooms, passed from one generation of Willinghams to another." David nodded, looked down and frowned as something caught his eye. He bent and scooped up the broken base of one of the cupids. " 'Made in Taiwan,' " he read, with a lift of his eyebrows. Smiling politely, he handed the bit of porcelain to a crimson-faced Clare. "As I said, Ms. Willingham, buy yourself some new 'heirlooms' and send the bill to my firm."

"David," Stephanie hissed, "I told you, it isn't necessary. I can repay Clare for the figures."

"When?" Clare demanded.

"Yes," David said evenly. "When?"

"Well—well, I'll contact her, as soon as I'm settled."

"As soon as you have a place to live," he said, his voice hardening, "and some money to buy groceries, you mean."

Stephanie flushed. "Where I live, and how, is no one's concern but mine."

"It's the court's concern," David said sharply, "or it should have been. Your lawyer must have been sitting on his brain when he argued this case."

"Dammit, I don't want to discuss this! I made my living as a secretary before. I can do it again.

I'll go to—to Atlanta. I'll get a job and I'll reimburse Clare down to the last penny.''

That was when it came to him. The idea was simple, obvious and logical, when he thought about it. It was an excellent, if temporary, solution to more than one problem—assuming he ignored the voice shouting, *Are you nuts?* inside his head.

''You're right,'' he said. ''You'll reimburse her.''

Stephanie nodded. He could tell, from the look on her face, that she'd been prepared for more argument.

''Well, I'm glad we agree.''

''I'll tell payroll to advance you your first month's pay, and you can send her a check.''

Her face went blank. ''What?''

David's hand curled around her elbow, the pressure of his fingers firm. ''It's not an unusual procedure,'' he said, knowing that it was an impossible one. Russell, Russell, Hanley and Chambers offered many benefits to its employees, but acting as a bank was not one of them. ''After all, now that we've found you a good job—''

''We have?''

''As my secretary.''

Stephanie's mouth dropped open. ''As your...''

"My secretary. Exactly."

"No! David—"

"And," he said, his eyes warning her not to try and defy him, "now that I've had time to think about it, I'm advising you to leave your clothing right where it is."

Stephanie's look changed from one of confusion to outright disbelief. "Why on earth would I do that?"

"Well," he said, "I could invent some legal mumbo-jumbo by way of explanation, but the simple fact is that I'd imagine it'll be an endless source of amusement for you, envisioning Ms. Willingham trying to shoehorn her corpulent self into your things."

There was a second of silence. Then Clare called David a name that made his eyebrows shoot into his hairline, and Stephanie laughed.

She had, he thought, a wonderful laugh. It was free, and easy, and when he looked at her, he suddenly had the feeling that this was the first time she'd laughed, really laughed, in years.

"Stephanie?" he said, and held out his hand.

Stephanie looked at his hand. She thought of her sad old suitcase, lying open on the bed upstairs, and that the only clothes in this entire house that were salvageable and really hers were the ones she was already wearing.

"Stephanie?" David said again, "shall we leave?"

Don't be stupid, she told herself, Stephanie, don't be an idiot...

"Yes," she said, and she smiled, took his outstretched hand, and walked away from Seven Oaks, and Clare, and the terrible memories of a life she'd never, ever wanted.

The day had started with soft breezes and bright sunshine, but as they drove away from Seven Oaks, it began to drizzle. By the time they reached the highway, the drizzle had turned into a downpour.

Stephanie sat rigid and silent, the euphoria of her departure gone. *What have I done?* she kept thinking, and when David turned on the windshield wipers, they offered not an answer but a command.

Go back, they sang as they swooped across the glass. *Go back, Stephanie, go back.*

"How about some music?" David said.

She jumped at the sound of his voice. He hadn't spoken a word until now, either. She looked at him, at the stern mouth and firm jaw. He was a man accustomed to getting what he wanted.

Out of the frying pan, into the fire, Steffie. Go back, go back, go back.

"Stephanie?"

Music. He was asking her if she wanted to hear—

"Yes." She swallowed dryly. "Music would be fine."

He reached out and punched a button on the dashboard. Dark, deep chords and arpeggios resonated through the car.

"Sorry," he said quickly, and punched another button. Rachmaninoff gave way to Paul Simon. "I like classical stuff, but, I don't know, at the moment, Rachmaninoff seems..."

Melodramatic, at the very least. Stephanie folded her hands tightly together in her lap. Here she was, fleeing one nightmare for what might just as easily be another.

"Do you like Simon? The old stuff, I mean, that he wrote and recorded with Art Garfunkel."

It was such an inane conversational thread; if she hadn't known better, she'd have suspected David was having second thoughts, too. But if he were, if he'd changed his mind about offering her a job, he'd have pulled off to the side of the road and told her so. Bluntly. If there was one thing she knew about David Chambers, it was that he didn't pull his punches. He said what he was thinking, took what he wanted without hesitation…

Her heart gave an unsteady thud. And she was running off with him?

The wipers swooshed across the windshield. *Oh, Steffie,* they sang. *Go back, go back, go back.*

Windshield wipers were strange things.

They swept across the glass, back and forth, back and forth, and after a while you could set a tune to them. Lyrics, too.

David's hands tightened on the steering wheel.

Unfortunately, he didn't much care for the words to this particular song. Not the one drifting from the car's speakers; Simon and Garfunkel were singing about Mrs. Robinson, and that was just fine. It was the lyric only he could hear that was the problem.

Cray—zee, the wipers sang, *Oh, man, you are crayay—zeeee…*

Damn right. How else to explain why he was driving along with Stephanie Willingham tucked into the seat beside him—although not even an optimist would describe her as looking ''tucked in.'' She looked about as relaxed as he felt. Her back was straight as a board, her hands were clenched in her lap, and her mouth was a tight little knot. People sitting in dental waiting rooms looked happier than she did, and who could blame her? He wasn't in the best of moods himself.

What in hell had possessed him? He'd gone down to Georgia because Jack had asked him to. Okay, maybe there'd been more to it than that. Maybe he'd gone to find what the shrinks called closure, a way of signing off on the experience of a couple of Sundays ago. Okay, so there was no "maybe" about it. He'd driven to Willingham Corners to take a cold look at Stephanie and get her out of his head. That had been step one. Step two was supposed to have been letting her bend his ear with her tale of woe, which would have led to the good part, when he chucked her under the chin and said, hey, he was sorry but she was fresh out of luck, and out of suckers...

Now here he was, top contender for the Sucker of the Year award.

Okay. Stephanie hadn't trapped him into this mess. Not directly. He'd managed to do that by himself. But she'd helped. Damn right, she had. David's jaw tightened. Instead of listening to Simon and Garfunkel, they ought to be humming strains from the *The Merry Widow*. That's what his passenger was, a widow who wouldn't even bother to pretend she was grieving, who claimed not to have a cent to her name or a job or a place to take shelter...

Claimed? It was probably true, otherwise she'd never have gone with him. So what? Those were her problems, not his. Stephanie had made her bed. Now she could lie in it.

Or in his. His bed. His arms. And he could kiss her until she went all soft and breathless, as she had before Clare had burst into the room, and perhaps then he could seek out and find that sweetness that seemed to be waiting just for him, only for him.

Cray—zee, the wipers blades whispered. *You are cray—zee...*

Think about the case. Concentrate on the law. What were the facts? Could a man leave his wife with zero bucks when he had plenty? Had Avery Willingham simply given Stephanie a raw deal? Had he bought her favor for cold, hard cash, married her, shown her off to the world but arranged it so that when he toddled off this planet, there was nothing for her to inherit?

But she was entitled to something, wasn't she? The court should have seen that.

On the other hand, how come Stephanie was broke? At the rate of a couple of thou per month, the little bride should have had time to amass a pretty decent retirement fund.

David frowned.

Where was the money? What had she done with it? It was a great question. How come he'd neglected to ask it?

David's frown deepened. Because he was the wrong person to handle this case, that was why. His involvement was too personal. Too—too something. Call it what you wanted, it was not going to work. A lawyer and a client worked best when there was some space between them, not when they started out with a history that involved damn near making it in the cabin of an airplane.

There was a way out. He'd get Stephanie to Washington, check her into a hotel and phone Jay O'Leary. Or Bev Greenberg. Or any of the half a dozen juniors at the firm. One of them would be more than happy to take the case, and, come to think of it, wasn't one of the pool secretaries going on maternity leave next week?

"That's it," David murmured.

"Excuse me?"

He looked at Stephanie. "Nothing," he said, and smiled. "Nothing at all."

Still smiling, he turned up the volume on the radio and began humming along with Paul and Art.

Nothing? Nothing at all?

Stephanie stared blindly out the window.

Something was going on in David's head, and she knew damn well it couldn't be classified as "nothing."

A few minutes ago, he'd looked like a man on his way to his own execution. Now he was the portrait of contentment, from his smug little smile to the fingers tapping against the steering wheel to the abominable, off-key humming. What did *he* have to feel so good about?

Nothing she could think of.

As for her, she was beyond feeling, unless you wanted to dwell strictly on the panic she felt growing inside her as the minutes, and the miles, flew by.

What on earth was she doing here? It had seemed such a wonderful exit, walking straight out the door of that hideous mausoleum and leaving Clare looking even more slack-jawed than usual.

So she'd done it. Shall we leave? this man—this arrogant, oh-so-quick-to-condemn man—had said. And she had. She'd followed him blindly and now here she was, heading for no place, with nothing to her name but the grungy clothes on her back, a handful of change that she'd scooped off her dresser this morning, and a comb.

Well, that's good, Steff. You have a comb, at least. That ought to be a big help when you get

*to D.C. and find out that this man has no real
intention of helping you. For all you know, he's
going to tell you that your "secretarial" duties
will begin, and end, in his bedroom.*

"Stop the car!"

David looked at Stephanie. She had a wild look
in her eyes and she was already fumbling with
her seat belt. He cursed, twisted the wheel hard
to the right and pulled onto the grassy shoulder
of the road. The car behind them shot past, horn
blaring.

"Dammit," he roared, "what the hell are you
doing?"

Flinging open the door, that was what she was
doing. Hurling herself out like a human projectile
and then sprinting for the nearby woods. David
undid his seat belt and chased after her.

She was easy enough to catch. Not that she
wasn't fast on her feet; it was only that he was
faster. Four years as a running back on a much-
needed football scholarship at Yale still guaran-
teed that. He reached her just as she entered the
treeline, tackled her and brought her down in a
tangle of arms and legs. They rolled down a shal-
low embankment and landed in a pile of last fall's
leaves, Stephanie on her back, David straddling
her.

"Dammit, Stephanie…"

"Don't you 'Stephanie' me, you—you—"

Words weren't enough. She made a fist and punched him, as hard as she could, in the belly. He grunted, grabbed for her wrists, forced her arms over her head and pinned them to the ground.

"Let go of me!"

"Not if you're going to pretend I'm a punching bag."

"Let—go—of—me, you—you..."

"Are you nuts? What did I do, to rate this?"

"You were born with the wrong chromosomes. Let go!"

"Will you behave if I do?"

"Yes," she said.

Only a fool would have believed her, and David had committed his last foolish act an hour ago, when he'd walked her out the door and into his life.

"You're pretty fast with the punches," he said as she struggled beneath him. "What'd you do, grow up in a gym?"

"No," she panted. "I grew up with a brother who believed in women being able to defend themselves against men like you!"

"Men like me?" David gave a short, sharp laugh. "Yup, you're right. You sure as hell need to know how to defend yourself against an s.o.b.

like me. Why, just look at what I've done in the past hour. Defended you against—''

''You didn't defend me,'' Stephanie huffed, trying to shove his weight off her. ''Why would you? I don't need defending.''

''Need it or not, I defended you. And I offered you free legal advice—''

''Some advice. You told me I've got as much chance of getting anything out of the estate as a—a cottonmouth has of getting petted.''

''It was not only free advice, it was excellent advice. Plus, I gave you a job.''

''Ha.''

''Listen, lady, maybe typing letters isn't half as exotic as what you used to do to earn your daily bread, but most women in your position would be grateful for it.''

''And what is *that* supposed to mean, huh? 'Most women in my position'? Just what, exactly, is *my* position, Mr. Chambers?''

It was a question fraught with many possibilities but, just then, David could only see one of them. Stephanie's position was directly under his, and even though he was angry, even though hanging on to her was like hanging on to a football at the bottom of a pileup, he knew suddenly that if she kept moving the way she was, they were both going to be in trouble.

"Okay," he said, "here's what I'm going to do."

"Oh, I know what you're going to do," Stephanie said fiercely.

"I'm going to stand up," David said, ignoring her. "Take it nice and easy, understand? Then we'll talk."

"We are done talking! I should never have listened to you in the first place. Walking me right past Clare and out of that house, and I never stopped to ask why!"

"I'm a sucker for appeals from the SPCA, too," David said grimly. "Dammit, don't do that!"

"You're no better than Avery, you—you liar!"

"Did he lie to you? Your husband?"

"Don't call him that," Stephanie said through her teeth. "And yes, he lied to me. I told you that. He said—he said he'd take care of my—my needs as long as it was necessary, but he didn't."

"What needs?" David said softly, and suddenly everything around them seemed to stop.

Stephanie looked up into David's face. His eyes were sapphire dark and locked on hers. The rest of him was locked on her, too. Chest to chest. Hip to hip. Thigh to thigh...

Warmth suffused her skin. Her heart gave an unsteady thump. Desperately, she tried to dislodge him.

"Don't..." David caught his breath. "Don't do that."

"Do what? Dump you on your head? Damn you, David!"

"That," he said, biting back a groan as she moved again. "Hell, that. You're the one who was busy talking about all those male chromosomes. What must I do, draw you a diagram?"

His body gave up the struggle and reacted to hers. He saw comprehension dawn in her eyes and she went absolutely still.

That had stopped her, he thought grimly. She wasn't fighting him anymore...not that he was thinking about her fighting him. All he could think about now was her softness. Her heat. Her scent.

"Let go," she said.

He would. He'd let go of her wrists, gather her into his arms and take her angry mouth in a long, hungry kiss—except, she wasn't angry. She had a look to her he'd seen in the eyes of a stray cat he'd found haunting the back alley when he was a kid, a cat so feral and afraid it had never let him get close enough to help it.

"Let me up," she said. "Right now."

The words were strong, but that didn't disguise the fear. Hell, it was more than that, it was something he didn't even want to put a name to. He drew back, his hands still holding hers.

"I'm not going to hurt you."

"Just—just get off me."

Her eyes glittered with unshed tears. He took a deep breath and fought against the unreasonable desire to kiss those tears away.

"Promise me you won't run?"

She nodded stiffly.

"Let me hear you say it. Tell me you're not going to run like a scared rabbit."

"I was not running like a scared rabbit."

He decided against arguing the point. He released her, rolled off her and stood up. He held out his hand, but Stephanie ignored the gesture, rose on her own and began dusting off her jeans.

"Maybe you'd like to tell me where you thought you were going," he said.

She sniffed, wiped her nose on her sleeve, and shrugged.

"Home."

"Home," he repeated.

His tone incredulous. Not that she could blame him. Where was home, exactly? It was just that anywhere was safer than here, when she didn't

trust this stranger or his promises...when she
didn't trust herself when he touched her.

"That's right. Home. I told you. Home. To
Willingham Corners."

"Ah, yes. Willingham Corners. And that
house." David folded his arms and fixed her with
an interested look. "How stupid of me. Come to
think of it, didn't the Yankees burn Tara?"

She gave a choked little laugh. "It's true. I
thought of Tara, too, the first time I saw Seven
Oaks."

David smiled. "When I rang the doorbell,
that's what I half expected to hear. Dah-daaah-
dah-dah...you know. That music."

"You almost did," Stephanie said. "For a
time, Avery actually thought about it."

"But you managed to talk him out of it?"

"Me? Talk Avery out of something?" Her
laugh was without humor this time. "I didn't
even try. He just got sidetracked, I guess. Not that
it mattered to me. It was his house, not mine."

"Strange way to feel, about a house that's your
home, isn't it?"

"Seven Oaks was never my home. It belonged
to my husband, and I...I..." Her voice trailed
away.

"And you belonged to him, too."

Anger flashed in her eyes. "Are we back to that?"

"We never left it."

"What do you want me to say, David? That it wasn't an arrangement I was proud of? Okay. It wasn't." Her shoulders slumped. "Look, I don't expect you to understand."

"Try me."

"I...I don't see how it matters."

"If I'm going to represent you," he said, waving a mental goodbye to his junior partners because, hell, this case was too complex for them, "the arrangement you keep referring to matters a great deal. I need to know the specifics."

"You know them. Avery deposited money in my name each month—"

"Did your sister-in-law hate you from the beginning?"

Stephanie shrugged. "No more than anyone else in town."

David nodded. "I got that feeling from the documents I read. And yet, you were going back there, where Clare's probably already changed the locks, and the good townsfolk are probably holding a party to celebrate the removal of the grasping, scheming, hard-hearted widow of the town's fair-haired patriarch."

"You don't believe in pulling your punches, do you, Mr. Chambers?"

"We've made too much progress to go back to such formality now, Mrs. Willingham. And no, I don't believe in pulling my punches. That is how they see you, isn't it?"

Stephanie lifted her chin. "Everyone does. Including you."

David reached out and plucked a leaf from her hair. "Change my opinion, then."

"How? By listing my virtues?" She drew herself up. "I am not about to defend myself to you or anybody, sir."

He smiled. "I like the way you say that."

"Say what?"

"Sir." His smile tilted. "It's very old fashioned, and polite—and yet, I get the feeling what you're really doing is calling me a four-letter word." He reached out and took another bit of leaf from her hair, his hand lingering against the dark curls. "Avery wasn't a nice guy, was he?"

"He was a rat," Stephanie said in a whisper.

"Because he cut you off without a cent?"

"Because he lied," she said sharply. "He lied about everything, and once I was trapped, once I realized, he just laughed and said I'd have to live with it."

She spun away, her arms wrapped around herself. David turned her to face him.

"Did he hurt you?"

She looked up. His eyes had gone as flat as his voice.

"He didn't beat me, if that's what you mean." She shook her head. "He was just—he got his kicks out of inflicting other kinds of pain. He was mean-tempered. Vindictive. He must have been the kind of little boy that pulled wings off bugs, you know?" She touched the tip of her tongue to her lips. "I suspect lots of people would agree, if it didn't mean bucking Clare and siding with me. Most folks would sooner shake hands with a rattlesnake than admit to having anything in common with Bess Horton's girl."

David's gaze swept over her face. It was bright with defiance.

"Is that your maiden name? Horton?"

She nodded.

"And what is it people have against your mother?"

Stephanie looked down and brushed a speck of dirt he couldn't see off her jeans.

"They don't have anything against her, anymore," she said brusquely. "She's gone."

"Gone where?"

She shrugged. "I've no idea."

"And the brother you mentioned? Where is he?"

"He's..." She hesitated. "He's around."

"Why didn't you leave Avery Willingham, if he was such a bastard?"

"I didn't know what he was like. Not at first. And besides..."

"Besides, there was the money." His tone was cold and accusatory.

"Yes," she said, so faintly that he had to strain to hear it.

"And it's all gone," he said.

She nodded.

"How? How could it be gone? What did you do with it?"

"I spent it."

"All of it? On what?"

"That's none of your—"

"Do you want me to represent you, or don't you?"

She stared at him. "Why would you do that? You don't like me. You don't believe anything I say. Why would you take me on?"

"Because I'm a lawyer," he said quickly. Too quickly. What was he getting into here? Nothing he couldn't get out of, he told himself, answering his own question. "And I believe that every person in this country is entitled to the protection of the law.''

''I couldn't pay you.''

''Our office does pro bono work all the time,'' he said, trying to think straight. It wasn't easy. She was touching the tip of her tongue to her bottom lip again. Her tongue was a pale, velvety pink, and her mouth was—her mouth was— ''But I need some answers first. Like, what happened to the money in your account?''

Stephanie thought of Paul, who'd been her courage and her strength when the town had pointed its fingers at Bess Horton and her dirty-faced, ragamuffin offspring. Who'd raised her, after their mother left. Who sat now in his room at Rest Haven, unable to do the things he used to do, and of the pride that was all he had left.

Swear to me, Steff, he'd said, *swear you won't ever tell anybody about me.*

She swallowed dryly and looked at David. ''I spent the money.''

''Gambling?'' She shook her head. ''Drinking?'' She shook her head again. ''Do you do coke? Heroin? Dammit, Scarlett.'' He shook her, hard. ''It couldn't have just trickled through your fingers.''

''It's gone,'' she said, her eyes on his. ''That's all I can tell you.''

"And now you want more," he said softly.

"I want what's rightfully mine. What Avery promised me."

It was the answer David had expected. Only a miracle would have made her say that she didn't want anything, now that she'd met him. Nothing but him, his kisses, his arms around her...

He stepped back, his hands curling into fists that he buried in his pockets, his anger as much for himself as for her.

"I'll take you to D.C.," he said. "To my place." He almost laughed at her strangled yelp of indignation. "There's a housekeeper's apartment in my town house. Bath, bedroom, small sitting room—and a lock on the door. All that's missing is a housekeeper. Mine sleeps out, not in."

"And what will you expect in return?" she asked coldly.

"Your presence at my office, five days a week from nine to five."

"Why are you doing this for me, David?"

He thought again of the stray cat he'd tried to help, all those years ago.

"It's for me," he said briskly. "Your case is interesting. Well?" He held out his hand. "Deal?"

Stephanie drew a deep breath. What choice was there? Slowly, she placed her hand in his.

"Deal," she said.

David's fingers closed around hers. Shake her hand, he told himself, do it in an impersonal way...

But his arms were already gathering her to him and she was yielding, melting, soft and warm as honey, into his embrace. He kissed her, kept kissing her, while time stopped. And when he finally let her go, he looked at his watch, then said, in a voice so calm that it amazed even him, "We'd better get moving."

David started for the car. Stephanie stood motionless.

Go back, the voice within her whispered.

He turned and looked at her. "Well?" His tone was brusque, almost impatient. "Are you coming?"

Steffie, don't do this...

Stephanie nodded. "Yes," she said, and followed him.

CHAPTER NINE

THE arrangement wasn't going to work.

Once again, David sat in his office, his back to his desk and his gaze fixed blankly on the cherry trees that lined the walk. The pink blossoms were falling almost as fast as his disposition, but then, it wasn't often a man had to admit defeat.

What had ever possessed him to think his crazy scheme had any chance at success?

Poverty was the curse that had been passed from one generation of Chamberses to the next, not insanity. And yet, he'd behaved like a certifiable lunatic. What else could you call a man who saw a woman he knew he shouldn't want, wanted her anyway, and told himself it wouldn't be any kind of problem to bring her into his life? Into his office? Hell, into his home?

David muttered a word that would have curled Miss Murchison's hair, if she'd been around to hear it. But, mercifully, Murchison was gone— and Stephanie was all too torturously here. After six days—five and a half, if you wanted to be exact—he was ready to admit that he'd made one huge mistake.

It had seemed so simple. Install Stephanie in the small apartment in his town house. Hire her as his secretary. See her in the office, where she'd at least make no more a mess of things than the memorable Miss Murchison, not see her at all at home, because the apartment had its own private entrance, as well as an entrance just off the kitchen...

"Great plan," David said to the cherry trees... except, something had gone wrong between the planning and the execution.

On the surface, things were going fine. Much to his surprise, Stephanie was as good a secretary as she'd claimed. His office had been transformed. His files were all up to date, his appointment calendar was accurate, the notes he scribbled during meetings or court proceedings were typed and organized so quickly it made his head spin. He'd even given up brewing his own coffee. Why wouldn't he, when Stephanie's was so much better?

She was pleasant to have around, too. Everybody said so, from the kid in the mail room straight up to the partners. Even Jack Russell, whose shocked expression made it clear he'd swallowed a mouthful of objections on learning the identity of David's new secretary, had admitted that much.

"Great improvement over the Grump," Jack had commented, "but—"

"I know all the 'buts,'" David had said, with the easy air of a man who was convinced he'd thought a problem through and solved it. "Not to worry, Jack. It's temporary."

"Temporary," Jack had replied thoughtfully, and David had nodded.

"Temporary, and practical."

"In that case," Jack had said with a smile, "I'll save my comments until you ask to hear them."

David scowled and turned his chair away from the window.

He could only imagine what Jack's comments would be if he knew that Stephanie wasn't only working for him but that she was living with him. Living under his roof, anyway. He hadn't lied about that part of it, he simply hadn't mentioned it because he'd known how that bit of information would have been received.

"There's no need to talk about our living arrangements," he'd told her gruffly, when they'd reached his home in Georgetown last Saturday.

"I'm not a fool, David," she'd said coolly. "People will talk, as it is. You may find this difficult to believe, but my reputation is as important to me as yours is to you.''

''It isn't that. It's just—I wouldn't want it to seem as if—''

''No. Neither would I.''

''Dammit,'' David said, and rose to his feet.

All he'd done was give a job and a place to live to a woman who needed them. The loan of some money, too, so she could show up at work in something other than a pair of jeans and a sweatshirt. He'd have done as much for anybody else in the same situation...

Who was he kidding? He'd come within inches of compromising his professional ethics. You didn't give a woman legal advice, employ her, take her into your home and all the time, every damn minute of every night and every day, want to take her in your arms and make love to her, without knowing you were walking a painfully fine line between what was right and what was wrong.

He never saw her, except in the office. Stephanie left before he did each morning, because she insisted on taking public transportation to work.

''Don't be stupid,'' he'd said brusquely. ''I'll drive you.''

''And do what? Drop me off a block away?''

"Well," he'd said, "well…"

"I can manage on my own, thank you. And I'll be punctual."

She was that. She was at her desk, ready to work the second he came through the door.

"Good morning, Mr. Chambers," she'd say, and she never so much as smiled or paused to say a word that wasn't business-related after that, even though he—even though he…

David mouthed another oath, jammed his hands into his trouser pockets and paced the length of his office.

She left at the end of the day, meaning she left only when he finally said, "Go home, Mrs. Willingham."

"Yes, sir," she'd say, and he'd sit in his office with the door partly open, watching as she straightened up her desk, collected her purse and perhaps a light sweater, then went out into the twilight. He had to force himself to sit still and not follow after her. There was no point. He'd tried that, the other evening after they'd worked an hour late.

"I'll drive you home," he'd said briskly, but Stephanie had shaken her head.

"Thank you, but I prefer going home alone."

The way she'd phrased it had been like a slap in the face. He'd felt a thrum of anger deep in his bones. For one crazy second, he'd thought of pulling her into his arms, kissing her until that cool smile left her mouth and her heart raced against his.

The windshield wipers had been right. He'd been crazy to do this, crazier still if he went on doing it.

Okay, then. He'd keep her on as his secretary. For a while, anyway. But he'd find her a different place to live. Someplace where he didn't have to lie awake nights, thinking of her sleeping just a few doors away. Where he didn't have to step into the hall in the morning and catch the faint whiff of her perfume. Where he didn't have to be strained to the limit by her presence.

"To the freaking limit," he said under his breath.

It had been fine, that first evening. Things had been brisk. Businesslike. He'd handed her the keys, pointed her toward the apartment, told her she was free to change things around as she liked and not to hesitate to let him know if she needed anything, and then he'd turned his back and walked away.

"No problem," he'd told himself smugly.

And there hadn't been. Not until somewhere around three or four o'clock, when he'd awakened from a dream hot enough to have left his heart pounding and his mouth dry...a dream in which Stephanie had starred.

It hadn't helped when he'd been shaving the next morning and he'd heard the faint hiss of water in the pipes. What was that? he'd wondered—and then he'd known. It was the shower running in her apartment.

"So what?" he'd said out loud.

The answer, to his chagrin, had come at once, in the mental image of Stephanie, wrapped in a towel, her skin dewy, her hair wet and curling around her face.

The swiftness of his physical reaction had both stunned and angered him. Hell, what was this crap? He wasn't some half-baked kid, operating at the mercy of runaway hormones. He was an adult male, fully in control of his own life. Rational. Intelligent. Pragmatic.

David rubbed his hand over his forehead. If he'd been any of those things, he'd never have gotten into such a mess. He'd have gone to Seven Oaks, delivered his message, and headed home. Okay, maybe he'd have offered to check out the subtleties of inheritance law or suggested an attorney she might contact...

"David?"

"What?" he snarled, swinging toward the door. Jack Russell stood in the opening, eyebrows lifted in inquiry.

"I knocked, David, but there was no answer. Are you all right?"

David blew out his breath. "I'm fine."

"Are you sure? If this isn't a good time, I can come back later."

"No, it's fine." He smiled, or hoped he did. "Come on in."

Russell shut the door behind him. "I just wanted to touch bases, let you know that the UPT deal went through, as you'd said it would." Jack shook his head as he looked around David's office. "Amazing. I just can't get over it. Your Mrs. Willingham. Such a remarkable find. She's been here only a week and look at what she's accomplished."

"A great deal. But she's not *my* Mrs. Willingham."

"Ah. Simply a figure of speech, I assure you. It *is* amazing, though. Five short days, to have done so much. Such efficiency. And so unexpected, in such an attractive package. Altogether, quite a remarkable find."

David leaned back against his desk, arms folded. "So you already said."

"And so I'm saying again. Truly, David, this is, well, it's—"

"Amazing."

"Yes."

"And remarkable."

"Yes, that, too. And—"

"Unexpected. Where are we going with this?"

Jack's brows rose again. "With what? I merely said—"

"You said it all a minute ago."

"So? Can't I repeat myself? As my ol' granpappy used to say…"

"Uh-huh."

"Anythin' worth sayin' is worth sayin' twice. Well, I'm saying it twice. The lady's talents are outstanding."

"Are you forming a chapter of the Stephanie Willingham Fan Club?"

Jack laughed, walked to one of the leather love seats, and sat down.

"My, oh, my, counselor. We are testy today, aren't we?" He undid the buttons on his vest, sighed and folded his hands in his lap. "In that case, perhaps I should follow granpappy's advice and cut to the chase."

David smiled tightly. "Granpappy and I agree, for once. Please do."

"Here it is, then. There's talk. And please, David, do us both the courtesy of not asking, talk about what?"

David's eyes narrowed. "I'm afraid you have me at a disadvantage, Jack. I *do* have to ask. Talk about what?"

"About her. Stephanie."

"What is there to talk about? I thought the consensus was that she's doing a good job."

"An excellent job." Russell lifted his hand and examined his fingernails. "The talk isn't about her work, David."

David leaned away from the desk. "Talk is cheap, Jack. You should know that."

"Yes, but is it true?" Russell looked up, the air of affability gone. "Is she living in your house?"

"Yes," David said coldly. "She is."

"My God, David…"

"Did whomever's busy spreading gossip bother adding that she's living in a separate apartment?"

Russell shook his head in dismay. "I don't believe this! How could you put yourself in such an untenable position? I didn't say anything when you brought her to the office, but—"

"I hired her to do a job."

"But taking her to live with you—"

"She isn't living with me! She's living in an apartment that happens to be located in my house."

"Surely, you must realize how this looks." Russell got to his feet. "For heaven's sake, man—"

"And even if she were living with me, the day I have to ask you or anybody else to vote on what in hell I do with my personal life is the day—"

"Whoa. Calm down. I'm not questioning your personal life. I'm questioning your sanity, and please don't tell me you don't see any problem with people thinking that you're sleeping with your secretary—a secretary whose reputation has preceded her."

"Listen, here, Jack..." David glared at the older man—and then he groaned, sank into the chair behind his desk and buried his head in his hands. "I've made a total screwup of this thing."

"Yes," Russell said gently, "you have, indeed."

David looked up. "I'm not sleeping with Stephanie," he said quietly. "You, of all people, should have known I wouldn't muddy the waters that way."

"I never thought you were, but not everyone in this office is so clear-minded about these things. Apparently, somebody noticed that the home address she gave on the employment forms is the same as yours, and…well, you know. People talk.''

''Yeah.'' David let out a deep sigh. ''She said they would.''

''She was right.'' Jack nodded toward a file on David's desk. The name ''Stephanie Willingham'' was scrawled across the cover. ''Have you taken her on as a client? I thought we'd agreed—''

''We didn't 'agree,' Jack. You said this case wasn't to our liking. Anyway, I've only been doing some research.''

''And?''

''And, Willingham and his sister dotted all the i's and crossed all the t's. Her chances of getting a piece of that estate are nonexistent.''

''Well, then…''

''She's broke. Penniless. I couldn't turn my back on her.''

''Yes.'' Russell smiled faintly. ''Just as I said, do you remember? There's a certain vulnerability to her. But you can't take her on as your private charity, David.''

David's expression turned cool. ''Are you trying to tell me whom I can and cannot employ?''

''No. Of course not.''

''That's good. That's damn good.''

"I'm telling you that I think you've shown an error in judgment, moving this woman into your home."

"When she can afford another place, she'll get one."

"You're making a mistake, David."

"It's my mistake to make, Jack."

"Slow down, will you? I'm not trying to tell you how to run your life."

"Aren't you?"

"David, I'm not a fool. I know you're the reason half of Washington thinks of us first when they think of a topflight law firm."

"Don't patronize me, Jack. I don't like it."

"I'm not patronizing you, I'm speaking the truth."

"What is it, then? You can't have grown so complacent that you're afraid the firm will be embarrassed—"

"Dammit, David! You're not talking to a wet-behind-the-ears kid here, with his eyes fixed on the Holy Grail!" Jack shook his head. "I'm concerned about you. You, the man. Not you, the attorney."

"There's nothing to be concerned about."

"I think there is. And I feel responsible. I was the one who got you into this mess. Why, you'd never have laid eyes on this woman if I hadn't—''

''I'd already laid eyes on her,'' David said abruptly, ''two weeks before you mentioned her name, and before you ask, no, I do not want to explain what I'm talking about.''

''David, my boy—''

''I'm not your boy, Jack. I'm not anyone's 'boy.' I'm a grown man, and while I appreciate your concern, what I do with my life is my affair.''

''Oh, hell. Mary warned me I'd do this all wrong. Look, I don't care about cheap gossip around the coffee machine. I care about you, David. I love you like a son. I just don't want to see you hurt by a woman who—a woman who—'' Jack threw his arms wide. ''Dammit, man, I don't even know how to describe Stephanie!''

David looked into the face of his old friend and mentor. Suddenly his anger drained away. He got to his feet and came around his desk.

''That's all right, Jack,'' he said quietly. ''I don't know how to describe her, either.''

The two men looked at each other for a few seconds. Then Russell smiled and clapped David on the shoulder. They walked slowly toward the door.

"Just don't get yourself in too deep, okay?"

David almost laughed. How deep was that? he wanted to say. Any deeper, he'd drown.

"Not to worry," he said lightly. "I'll know when it's time to bail out."

"You want some last advice?"

David smiled. "No. But that won't stop you from giving it."

"The lady's beautiful, bright, and broke. And okay, maybe she got a raw deal. But do yourself a favor. Write her a glowing letter of recommendation, hand her a copy of the employment ads, and say goodbye."

"I'll consider it."

"That's the spirit." Russell smiled. "I'm glad you'll be getting your mind off all this for the weekend."

"What about the week..." David clapped his hand to his forehead. "Damn! The Sheraton house party. I'd almost forgotten."

"Check your calendar. I'm sure the efficient Mrs. Willingham has it listed."

"Oh, hell. The last thing I feel like doing is taking on Mimi Sheraton."

"Interesting choice of words," Jack said, chuckling.

"An entire weekend, avoiding that barracuda."

Jack opened the door. "I keep telling you, my boy. What you need is an excuse even our Mimi can't ignore."

"Yeah. Like my name on the obituary page."

"Or on the society page. An announcement, that you're to be married." Jack winked. "Mary's advice, but I tend to agree."

"Tell Mary, thanks a bunch." David grinned. "Women just like to see men lassoed and branded. Well, not me. Once was more than enough."

Russell laughed. "Too bad you can't just phone that rental company we used for that Fourth of July party last year. You know, the one that rents dishes, chairs, tables…see if they have a division called Rent-A-Fiancée."

"Thanks, counselor," David said, smiling. "Be sure and send me a bill for your sage advice."

He was still smiling when he shut the door.

"Rent-A-Fiancée," he said as he strolled back to his desk. Too bad there wasn't such a thing. But he could try another approach. He could call one of the women he'd been seeing, invite her to go to the Sheratons with him. Yes, there was a down side to that. With his luck, the lady in question might end up thinking his intentions were more serious than they were, but it was worth a shot. Anything was better than spending the weekend trying to avoid Mimi and dark hallways—

"Mr. Chambers?"

David turned around. Stephanie looked at him from the doorway. God, how beautiful she was!

"Sir? Do you—can you spare a minute?"

He sighed. It was just as well. He supposed he had to tell her that the gossip had begun. She had the right to know.

"Of course," he said. "Come in and sit down, Mrs. Willingham."

Stephanie nodded, shut the door behind her and stepped into the room.

She hadn't wanted to do this.

David had done enough for her. A job, a place to live, a loan. She couldn't ask him. She couldn't. On the other hand, what choice was there? Rest Haven had phoned again last night. The director had been pleasant, but firm. She was already a month behind in payments. They couldn't wait any longer.

"Your brother's care is costly, Mrs. Willingham," the director had said.

As if she didn't know that already.

She knew it was useless but, during her lunch hour, she'd gone to the bank where she'd opened an account, and asked for a loan. To his credit, the loan officer hadn't laughed in her face. In desperation, she'd phoned Amos Turner. He hadn't been as kind. She'd hung up the phone, face burning, the sound of the lawyer's laughter ringing in her ears. And then she'd suffered the worst humiliation of all. She'd called Clare, who'd listened, let her talk on and on until she was near begging before Clare had laughed hysterically and hung up the phone.

So Stephanie had steeled herself for what had to be done. There was no other choice. She had to ask David to lend her the money.

"How much?" he said, with the kind of smile that suggested this was a joke.

"Five thousand," Stephanie said, with no smile at all. "I know it's an enormous amount of money, but I'll repay you the second you get me my share of Avery's—"

"Why in heaven's name do you need five thousand bucks?"

She hesitated. The bank loan officer had asked her the same question, in just the same tone of voice.

"I—I don't think that's important."

David laughed.

"You've got a lot of brass, Scarlett, I'll give you that much. Five thousand bucks, and it's not important?"

"It is. I mean, the amount is. And the reason I need it is. But—"

"But it's none of my business. Right?"

The tip of her tongue snaked out between her lips. He tried not to notice.

"I understand that you'd like some answers, David. But—"

"It doesn't matter." He sat down, leaned forward across his desk and folded his hands on the polished cherrywood surface. "I've gone over your case a dozen times, and I have to tell you, I can't see any way around the judge's decision."

Stephanie blanched. "But you said—"

"I said I'd give it my best shot. Well, I have. We could petition the courts, make a case for your having been left destitute." His eyes fixed on hers. "I could probably get you a couple of hundred a week for a year or two, long enough for you to get back on your feet."

"It isn't enough!" She could hear the thread of panic in her voice and she swallowed hard before she spoke again. "I need—"

"Five thousand dollars." His smile was remorseless. "I heard you the first time. Well,

Scarlett, I'm afraid you're just going to have to accustom yourself to a simpler lifestyle.''

''Dammit! I don't want the money to—to... I need it.''

His eyes went flat and cold. ''For what?''

''I can't—''

''You can,'' he said, and he reached out, clasped her wrist and rose to his feet. Defiance glittered in her eyes but her mouth was trembling. Jack was wrong, he thought. Vulnerable wasn't the word to describe her. He remembered the feral kitten, how it had spit and refused to be stroked...and yet, how clearly it had needed the gentling touch of a loving hand. He looked into Stephanie's beautiful face and thought, just for a moment, that he could see straight into her wounded soul.

''David?'' she whispered, and then she was in his arms. She gave a soft cry as he gathered her to him; her body sank into his. Her slender arms looped around his waist in a gesture that seemed equal parts desire and despair.

His heart hammered. He knew he had only to caress her, lift her into his arms, carry her to the love seat, and she would be his. But she had been Avery Willingham's, too. Would she belong to any man, for the right price?

He reached behind his back, grasped her wrists and drew her arms to her sides. It was the hardest thing he'd ever done in his life. Knowing that made him even angrier.

"Okay," he said, his voice harsh. "I get the message. You're broke, you need a bundle of cash, and you don't know how to get it."

He heard the indrawn hiss of her breath. "That's an oversimplification."

"Let's not argue the semantics of this, Scarlett, all right?" He cocked his head and looked at her. "Did you ever do any acting when you were in school?"

Stephanie stared at him as if he'd lost his mind. Hell, he thought, maybe he had.

"Acting?"

"Yeah. You know, playacting."

"I don't see what that has to do with anything."

"Humor me. Just answer the question."

"No. Well..." Her brow furrowed. "Well, once. In sixth grade. We did *Sleeping Beauty,* for spring assembly."

"Okay," he said briskly, as if what he was about to propose wasn't completely, totally, absolutely insane. "Okay, then, here's the deal." He walked away from her, to his desk, sat down behind it as if putting distance between them could make what came next sound like the rational suggestion of a rational man. ''I'm going to a house party this weekend, in the Virginia countryside. A client's hosting it. Lots of people networking, pretending to have a good time.'' He shot her a humorless smile. ''It's hard to explain, unless you've been to one of these things.''

''Buffet breakfasts on the sideboard,'' Stephanie said. ''Drinks around the fireplace. You don't have to explain. Avery was big on trying to impress the right people. But I still don't see—''

''My client's wife will have one other item on the agenda.'' David sat back, his eyes on Stephanie's. ''She's on the make.''

''David, I'm sorry, I'm just not following you.''

''She'll seat me next to her at dinner,'' he said bluntly, ''and while her right hand's holding her salad fork, her left will be searching for my lap.''

He thought, just for a second, that she was going to laugh. Her eyes widened; her mouth twitched. He remembered the last time—the only time—Stephanie had laughed, how wonderful it had made him feel, and he almost smiled…and then he remembered that she had just come to him for five thousand bucks, with no explanation other than that she needed it, and his smile faded before it began.

"So, I'm going to take Jack Russell's advice. He says my only salvation is to take my fiancée with me."

There wasn't even a hint of a smile on her lips now.

"Your... Well, of course. I'm sure he's right. A fiancée is certain to put you off-limits."

David nodded. The office seemed to fill with silence.

"There's only one problem. I don't have a fiancée. So here's my proposal. You need five thousand dollars, I need an actress. Sound workable to you?"

The color drained from Stephanie's face. "You mean, you want me to... You're joking!"

"I've never been more serious."

"No," she said quickly. "No, I couldn't."

"Sure you could." He got to his feet and walked toward her, moving slowly, his eyes never leaving hers. "All you have to do is pretend you're back in sixth grade."

"It wouldn't be right."

"Think of it as a kind of collateral on the loan, if it makes you feel better."

"David, it's crazy." Her eyes narrowed. "Are you figuring I'll go to this house party and sleep with you? Because if you are—"

"My motives are purely self-protective, Scarlett. Mimi Sheraton's husband's a nice guy. He deserves better than having me tell him what his wife's doing." Don't touch her, David told himself. It's bad enough you've made this crazy offer... But a stray curl lay against Stephanie's cheek, and he couldn't help it; he reached out and let it slip around the tip of his finger. "It wouldn't be so difficult, pretending you and I were lovers, would it?"

"David, this is crazy. You can't expect—"

He bent his head and kissed her. Nothing touched but their mouths and yet Stephanie felt something warm and sweet stir and spread its wings, deep in the hidden recesses of her heart.

He lifted his head, his eyes locked on hers. "Say you'll do it," he said gruffly, and he held his breath, waiting, until, at last, in a voice he could hardly recognize, she said that she would.

CHAPTER TEN

THE Sheraton house made Seven Oaks look like an impostor.

Not that the house was another Tara. David had told her it was a Virginia farmhouse, but when had a farmhouse looked like a cross between Buckingham Palace and the Taj Mahal?

"I'll bet nobody with manure on his boots ever got further than that porch," Stephanie murmured as David took their luggage from the back of his Porsche.

David's brow lifted. "Manure, Scarlett?"

"Manure, David. I'm sure you'll be amazed to hear we have our fair share of the stuff back home in Georgia."

He grinned. "Not quite as much as there is in our esteemed capitol, but why quibble? You're right. The only thing rural about this place is Mimi's little speech to newcomers about the purity of the bucolic ethos she demanded of her architect and interior designer."

Stephanie laughed. "She doesn't really say that!"

"Heck, for all I know, she might be right— assuming the *ethos* of a Virginia farm in the seventeen hundreds included gold faucets in all the johns, a dining room that seats fifty, and hot and cold running servants." David hoisted both their overnight bags under one arm. "Here comes one now. Just watch."

Stephanie looked toward the house again. A young man dressed in a white jacket and dark trousers was coming briskly toward them.

"Welcome to Sheraton Manor, madam. May I help you with your luggage, sir?"

"Thank you," David said, "but I can manage myself."

"I'm sure you can, sir, but—"

"James," David said. "Your name *is* James, isn't it? I believe we went through a similar dance the last time I was here."

"Yes, sir. I mean, my name is James, sir. And I—"

"And you are here to anticipate my every need." David smiled and clapped a hand on James's shoulder. "The thing of it is, James," he said conversationally, "I had a job picking up after people when I was just about your age."

James stared at him. "You, sir?"

"Me. And when I finally had enough money to quit, I promised myself I'd never, in this lifetime, ask any man to do something for me that I was capable of doing for myself. Can you understand that, Jimmy?''

For an instant, a boy seemed to replace the proper young man.

''I certainly can...sir.''

David smiled and held out his hand. There was a bill tucked inside it. ''Glad we understand each other, son.''

The boy's eyes widened. ''Yes, sir. And I hope you have a very pleasant weekend. You and your lady both.''

Stephanie, who'd been smiling at this exchange, suddenly frowned. ''I am not—''

''I'm sure we will.'' David took her arm. ''Won't we, Scarlett?''

Their eyes met and held, and finally she nodded stiffly. ''Yes.''

David smiled. ''See you around, Jimmy,'' he said, and he headed toward the house, his hand still clasping Stephanie's.

''You don't have to hang on to me,'' she said coldly. ''I'm not going to run away.''

''You're not going to convince Mimi Sheraton that you and I are an item, either, despite what I told her on the phone. Not if you turn to stone each time someone refers to us as a couple.''

''He said—James said—''

"That you were my lady."

"Yes. And I'm not."

David stopped, dropped the suitcases and spun Stephanie toward him. "Let's get the ground rules straight here, Scarlett. You've agreed to act the part of the woman I'm engaged to marry."

"I understand that." She glared at him. "That doesn't mean...I just don't like the way he said what he said. As if I were your—your—"

"My what?"

"I don't know." And she didn't. What had the boy said that was so terrible? What was the difference between being David's lady and his fiancée?

"He made it sound as if we were lovers," David said matter-of-factly.

Stephanie flushed.

"I suppose he did. And that isn't what we agreed to."

"I see."

"I hope you do, David, because—"

"This is damn near the twenty-first century, Scarlett, and we are both adults. If we were really engaged to be married, I can promise you, we'd be lovers."

"Fortunately for me, we are not *really* anything."

"Listen, Scarlett..."

"David! Yoo-hoo. David, here I am!"

David looked around. Stephanie did, too. A woman stood on the porch. Her auburn hair was lacquered into artful disarray, her makeup was impeccable, and her smile was brilliant.

"Oh, my," Stephanie whispered, "all she needs is a baton and a bathing suit!"

"Mimi," David said under his breath, and gave a quick wave of his hand.

"Sweetie, hurry on up here so I can say a proper hello!"

Stephanie's mouth twitched. "Sweetie?"

"Exactly," David said out of the side of his mouth. "And if you think Miss America's going to be put off by you, me, and chastity, you'd better think again."

"I'm not going to sleep with you," Stephanie said quickly.

His smile sent a wave of heat curling straight down to her toes. "Is that a dare, Scarlett?"

"It's a statement of fact, Rhett."

"David?" Mimi waggled a coral-taloned finger in their direction. "Are you going to make me come down to you?" She laughed and tossed her head, but not one hair so much as shifted. "You know what the sun does to my skin, sweetie."

Stephanie cocked an eyebrow. "Goodness to Betsy, *sweetie,* whatever does it do?"

"That's it," David said grimly.

"No," Stephanie said. "David—"

But he'd already pulled her into his arms. "Smile," he said. "Act as if you're enjoying this." And his mouth covered hers.

Act, he'd said...but she didn't have to act. Not when the touch of his lips sent her heart bumping against her ribs, when the earth tilted so that she had to curl her fingers into his jacket and hang on.

"You see?" he said, when he'd finished kissing her. His smile was as cool as if they'd done nothing more than shake hands. "You can carry this off, if you put your mind to it."

He picked up their luggage and took her hand, the pressure of his fingers exerting a clear message. Live up to our bargain, he was saying, or pay the penalty...and yet, if having him take her in his arms and kiss her was the penalty, did she really want to resist it?

Mimi Sheraton was all smiles as she greeted David, all girlish purrs as she air-kissed Stephanie on both cheeks, but neither the smiles nor the purrs disguised the fact that Stephanie was about as welcome at Sheraton Manor as she'd been at Seven Oaks.

Mimi tried to be subtle. She pushed herself between them, linked arms and led them into a foyer
big enough to double as a dance hall, playing the
role of perfect hostess to the hilt, chattering non-
stop as she led them up a wide staircase. They
paused at the top, and Mimi turned her smile on
Stephanie.

"You must tell me, dear. However did you
land this gorgeous man?"

"I'm afraid you'll have to ask him," Stephanie
said airily.

"It was all rather sudden, wasn't it?" Mimi
clutched their arms again and started down the
hall. "I mean, how long have you and David
known each other?"

Stephanie looked past their hostess to David for
help, but he was strolling along, seemingly intent
on studying the carpet that seemed to stretch for
miles into the distance.

"You must be the reason he hasn't been available the past couple of weeks," Mimi said, answering her own question. She flashed her killer
smile. "You know, darling, there are going to be
scores of ladies out for your scalp. Even I, a happily married woman, was stunned when David
phoned yesterday and told me the news."

Stephanie laughed gaily. "You'll defend me,
won't you, Mimi? As a happily married woman."

Mimi chuckled. "Of course! Ah. Here we are." She drew their little party to a halt and opened the door on a sea of blue. "The Blue Room for you, David, sweetie." She leaned toward him, batting her lashes. "I'm just across the hall, remember?"

David smiled politely. "How could I possibly forget?"

"And your girlfriend—"

"Fiancée."

"Fiancée. Of course. That's what I meant. She's in the Ruby Room in the West Wi—"

"No."

Mimi's smile faltered. "No?"

David looked down at Mimi's hand, clutching his elbow. Gently, he peeled it loose, moved to Stephanie's side, and put his arm around her.

"Scarlett and I wouldn't want to be separated, not even for one night. Would we, darling?"

"Scarlett," Mimi said with a little laugh, "isn't that charming?"

"Charming," Stephanie said through her teeth. She looked at David. "Of course we wouldn't want to be separated, lover. But if those are the arrangements our hostess has made..."

"Then," David said, "I'm afraid she'll just have to unmake them." He looked at Mimi. "That isn't a problem, is it?"

Mimi cleared her throat. "Well...well, I suppose...Scarlett—I mean, Stephanie can have the room next to yours."

"Do the rooms connect?"

Stephanie resisted the urge to slap that little smile from David's handsome face. "It really isn't necessary—"

"Yes, it is," David said, and kissed her.

Mimi made a strangled sound. "Cocktails in an hour," she chirruped, and fled.

Stephanie glared at her opened suitcase.

"I," she said to it, "am going home." All David's talk, about needing to thwart Mimi Sheraton's plans. "Liar," Stephanie muttered.

What did he think? That he'd purchased a playmate for the weekend? Well, he was in for one hell of a nasty surprise...although, it was true, Mimi did seem to have her sights set on David.

Stephanie sat down on the edge of the bed. Actually, even a trout snapping at a mayfly would have shown more finesse, but that didn't mean David had to make such a display of kissing her or of his intention of supposedly slipping into her bed tonight, when the house lay silent and sleeping.

Didn't he care what people thought?

Stephanie flopped back against the pillows. Of course, he cared. He *wanted* them to think exactly what Mimi was thinking. That was the purpose of all of this. And she had no right to complain. She'd agreed to play this dumb game. David was lending her five thousand dollars to go along with it, and who was she kidding? He was *giving* her the money because she'd probably be a hundred years old before she saved enough to pay him back.

Oh, lord. What a mess. She *hated* the way Mimi Sheraton had looked at her, *hated* the cheap way she'd felt...

Be honest, Steffie. What you really hate is how you crumple each time David kisses you.

She sat up. There was only one thing to do. She'd have to tell him this ridiculous deal was off. No playing his girlfriend.

No five thousand dollars.

What would become of Paul?

He had never turned his back on her, not even after their mother left. Not that Bess's leaving had made a difference. Bess hadn't paid much attention to either of them, and Stephanie had done the cooking, cleaning, washing and ironing ever since she could remember.

Paul was the one whose life had changed. He'd been forced to grow up fast. He'd quit school and become their breadwinner, and even though he was younger than she by eleven months, he'd turned into her big brother and father all in one. He'd even given up his music, the thing he loved most, rather than leave her alone to face Willingham Corners and the world it represented.

How could she have left *him*, after his accident? It hadn't even been much of an accident. His car skidded off the road one rainy night and hit a tree. The fender got crumpled and Paul got a bump on his head, but a few weeks later, he'd started to change. He began to have headaches, and hear noises, and sometimes he didn't know who she was or where he was...

''Swear to me, Steff,'' he'd begged when he was lucid. ''Swear you won't ever tell anybody what's happened to me. They'll say it's 'cause I'm a Horton, 'cause I'm our mama's son.''

So she'd sworn. And she'd never gone back on her word—except when, in desperation, she'd told Avery Willingham.

Stephanie rose to her feet. Paul needed her help, as she had once needed his. She didn't regret the sacrifice she'd made, marrying Avery, even though he'd lied when he'd promised to treat her like a daughter. It was this sacrifice that was the difficult one. Pretending to be in love with David was hard. No. That was wrong. The pretending wasn't hard. Why would it be? David was—he was... A woman would find it easy to love him. He was wonderful, everything she'd ever wanted, ever hoped and prayed for.

Stephanie's breath caught. No, she thought, no, please, no...

"No," she said, and hurried to the door that connected their rooms. She couldn't go through with this. She'd take a train, go to Rest Haven. She'd plead with the doctors. With the director. They'd understand. They had to, because she couldn't do this, couldn't spend this weekend with David, pretending to be his lover.

"David?" she called, and knocked on the door. "David, are you there?" She knocked again, waited, and then, carefully, she opened the door.

David's clothing lay strewn across the bed. Beyond, the bathroom door stood ajar. She could hear the sound of running water.

He was showering. Well, she'd sit down and wait until...until what? Until he walked, naked, into the room? Her heart banged into her throat. She could imagine how he'd look, his skin golden and glistening with drops of water, his hair loose around his face. He'd be magnificent to look at, broad-shouldered and lean-hipped, his muscles taut...

Stephanie fled to the safety of her own room, and locked the door behind her.

"Chambers, you lucky son of a gun!" The newest, youngest Supreme Court justice paused en route to the bar and slapped David lightly on the back. "You certainly have found yourself a winner."

"That I have," David said. He smiled and took a sip of his cognac. A winner, he thought, and took another sip. Maybe the cognac would take the edge off. Something had to, or he was going to explode.

The evening wasn't going quite the way he'd imagined.

It had seemed such a fine plan—telling Mimi he was engaged, bringing Stephanie along and making it clear he was out of circulation. He'd been so sure of its logic.

What an idiot he was.

Everything had seemed fine. Well, not fine, really. Kissing Stephanie hadn't been so clever. He'd done it for Mimi's benefit, but he'd been the one who'd ended up standing under a cold shower, thinking thoughts he knew better than to think, trying but not succeeding in not imagining what would happen if Stephanie climbed into the shower with him.

But the shower had helped. He'd cooled down, had a stern heart-to-heart with himself in the bathroom mirror as he'd shaved, gotten all spiffed up in his white dinner jacket and black trousers and marched to the door that led into Stephanie's room.

"All ready?" he'd said pleasantly when she'd opened the door…and that had been the end of him, because one look at her and he knew it was all over.

She was simply gorgeous.

There were other ways to describe how she looked, in a creamy slip of a dress with her hair loose and shining and hanging down her back, but why come up with a bunch of useless adjectives when one would do?

He'd sent her shopping in Georgetown, with instructions to buy whatever she thought would make Mimi Sheraton take notice.

"I'll repay the cost of whatever I purchase," she'd said stiffly, and he hadn't bothered arguing. What was the point, when she already owed him five thousand bucks and had to know, as he did, that she could probably never repay it?

But when he saw her, he knew it wasn't only Mimi who'd take notice, it would be every man on the premises.

''Will I do?'' she'd said as dispassionately as you'd ask somebody if they wanted their coffee black or with cream.

''Sure,'' he'd said with a shrug, while some evil presence in his primitive male brain urged him to grab her and drag her into his cave. His civilized brain argued that it didn't have to be a cave. His bed would do. But even in his demented state, he knew she wouldn't let him get away with it. So he'd compromised by pulling her into his arms and kissing her. She hadn't protested. He hadn't given her the chance, though it had pleased him, when the kiss ended, to see how her eyes glittered.

''Just wanted to be sure you had the right look,'' he'd said briskly, as if kissing her had been part of some careful plan, and then he'd put his arm around her waist and led her down to the party.

Half an hour later, he knew he'd made a mistake. Not in figuring the dampening effect Stephanie would have on Mimi. That seemed to be working just fine. David took a hefty swig of his cognac. No, his mistake had been in thinking he could bring Stephanie into a roomful of men, turn her loose and not go crazy watching what happened.

The men circled her like bees around the sweetest flower in the garden.

The jerk from *The Washingtonian* had damn near drooled into his cold sorrel soup. A lecherous congressman from California had all but dipped his tie into his blackened tuna. And when the fat cat financier from Boston had put his hand on Stephanie's, David had come close to grabbing him by the throat and telling him to back off because, dammit, she belonged to him.

All these s.o.b.'s thought she was his fiancée. They had no right to hover around her. She had no right, either, to laugh and listen with rapt attention to every stupid story they told. She had no right to have a good time with anybody but him. Didn't she know she was his? Well, supposed to be his. For the night. For the weekend. Hell, for as long as he wanted. Didn't she know that?

Just now, she was holding court with a group of men who pretty much ran the world, according to the American press, and they were lapping up her every word—including the congressman from California, who'd just casually slipped his arm around her waist.

David's eyes narrowed. He tossed back the rest of his cognac and put down the snifter.

"Easy," a male voice said.

He swung around. Tom Sheraton had come up beside him.

"She can handle things, that girlfriend of yours." Tom smiled. "But the sooner you put a wedding band on her finger, the sooner those fools will get the message."

"Yeah," David said through his teeth. "If you'll excuse me, Tom..."

"So, when's the happy occasion?"

"The? Oh. Well, we only just got engaged..." David frowned. The congressman whispered something in Stephanie's ear. She tossed back her head and laughed. "Uh, as I was saying, we just got engaged, so..." The syndicated political columnist standing on Stephanie's other side leaned in, too, and offered a comment. She smiled and turned toward him, at the same time neatly dislodging the old goat's arm. "As I was saying, we really haven't had time to..." Dammit, was there no end in sight? A movie star with a mane of blond hair, a thousand-watt smile and a penchant for the-cause-of-the-day, deftly shouldered the columnist aside and took Stephanie's arm. He said something, she nodded, and the two of them started toward the terrace.

Enough, David thought. "Great party, Tom," he said, and he strode up to Stephanie and lay a proprietorial hand on her shoulder.

"David," she said with a little smile, "have you met Gary?"

David looked at the actor. "No."

"Well, let me intro—"

"Stephanie, could I see you for a minute?"

Stephanie frowned. "Yes, but first—"

"I want to talk to you."

"I understand, David, but—"

"Forget the 'but's,' Scarlett." David clamped his arm around her waist. "You're coming with me, and now."

He saw the flash of anger in her eyes but he moved quickly, herding her out the door and onto the terrace before she could protest. His luck ran out as soon as they stepped outside; she twisted free of his arm and glared at him.

"What kind of performance was that?"

"You're the one who's been giving a performance, madam, starting with the hors d'oeuvres and working straight through the coffee and cake."

"I don't know what you're talking about." She stalked down the stone steps and into the garden, with him on her heels. "How dare you drag me off that way?"

"I did not 'drag' you off, though believe me, I was tempted." David grabbed her arm and spun her toward him. "Since when does a man have to beg his fiancée for a minute of her time?"

"I was talking to someone, or hadn't you noticed? Gary was telling me a funny story about something that happened on the set of his last film, and—"

"Gary," David said, "wouldn't know a funny story unless somebody pointed it in his direction and told it to bite him on the ankle."

"For your information, Gary not only acted in that film, he directed it. And wrote the script."

"A, a piece of wood shows more acting talent than he does. B, he couldn't direct a dog to lift its leg at the nearest tree, and C, can you really write a script with crayons?"

"Oh, that's hilarious, David. Very funny. And, by the way, I would remind you, I am *not* your fiancée."

"You are, for the weekend."

"And what a mistake that was," Stephanie said, blowing a curl out of her eyes.

David's gaze narrowed. "Meaning?"

"Meaning, I agreed to help you out of a tight spot. I didn't agree to become your property. Now, if that's all—"

David clamped a hand around her wrist as she started to turn away.

"Where do you think you're going?"

"To my room, to pack. I have decided to return to the city."

"No way, Scarlett. We made a deal, remember?"

"It was a bad one, and I am terminating it."

"You didn't quit when Avery Willingham bought your services."

He saw the color drain from her face and cursed himself for being a fool. That wasn't what he'd meant to say. The truth was, he didn't know what he'd meant to say. He only knew that it was safer to be angry at her than to admit the truth, that he was hurting because she'd ignored him all night and that the hardest thing he'd ever done in his life was to keep smiling while he shared her with a roomful of people.

"You're right," she said, "I didn't." Her voice trembled, but she met his eyes with unflinching determination. "I'm an honest whore, David. I sold myself to you and to him, and both times I got exactly what I deserved."

"Damn you," he growled. His fingers bit into her wrist and he moved closer to her. "I want some answers. Why, Scarlett? Why did you marry a man you despised?"

"This isn't the time."

"It damn well is. Tell me the truth."

''Please.'' She shook her head, grateful for the darkness of the night, knowing that what he saw in her eyes now could be her undoing. ''Let go of me, David. We both know this was a mistake. I'll pack my things and make some excuse to Mimi—''

''Scarlett. Look at me.''

She shook her head again but the pressure of his hand was persistent.

''I need to know the reason.'' He thought he could see the telltale glimmer of tears in her eyes, and he bent his head and brushed his lips over hers. ''Don't shut me out, Scarlett. Please. Let me help you.''

Silence filled the moment. It stretched between them, shimmering with a quality as ephemeral as the moonlight, and then the tears rolled down her cheeks.

''I have a brother.'' She spoke in a whisper; David had to lean closer to hear her words. ''My little brother. He's always been—he means everything to me, David. He's all I have, all I ever had, and—and he's ill. Terribly ill. He needs special care, and it costs a small fortune. Avery knew. He was wonderful. He helped me find the right place for Paul. He even lent me money for his care, but it grew more and more costly and eventually, Avery said—he suggested...''

She trembled, and David drew her closer.

"It's all right," he said softly.

"But it isn't. Don't you understand? I married Avery because he said—he said it was the only way he could guarantee Paul would always be cared for properly. He said he'd—he'd treat me as he always had, that he'd be my friend...." She shuddered. "He lied," she whispered. "About everything."

About everything. The words echoed in David's brain. God, what had Avery Willingham done to her?

"Sweetheart." He drew her close, stroked her hair as she buried her face against him. Her body was racked with sobs, and it broke his heart. "Sweetheart, don't cry."

She pulled back in his embrace and looked up at him, eyes wide, mouth tremulous.

"I was supposed to be his hostess. His companion. His social secretary. He said—he said he'd never touch me." She drew a deep, shaky breath. "But he lied. After a while, he—he came to my room..."

"Hush," David said, and told himself that wanting to beat the crap out of a dead man was possibly blasphemous and undoubtedly insane. "It's over now, Scarlett. Try and forget."

"And then, he died. And Clare came, and she laughed and laughed, and she told me Avery had never intended to leave me anything, that as it was, he'd kept me around longer than he'd intended, but it was only because he'd gotten sick—"

David kissed her. Her lips were cold, her skin icy, but he kept kissing her until he felt the warmth returning to her flesh.

"I know what you must think of me," she whispered. "But I trusted Avery. And I couldn't see any other way—"

"What I think," David said fiercely, "is that you're a fine, brave woman. And that I'm an idiot for making you cry."

"I should never have come with you this weekend. It was bad enough I let you give me a job, and a place to live. But going away with you..." Her eyes met his. "I wouldn't have slept with you, David."

"I know."

"My situation with Avery, wrong as it might have been, was different."

David nodded. "You were his wife."

"Yes. And I was a good wife, strange as that may sound. So you can see why I—why I can't live up to my end of our bargain." She swallowed hard, and tried not to think about where she could turn for the money she needed, nor about what it would be like, never to see David again. "I'm not for sale anymore."

His thumbs traced patterns along her cheekbones.

"I know," he said, as calmly as if he'd intended this, as if he weren't about to say something that would make everything he'd done up till now seem meaningless. "That's why I want to marry you."

CHAPTER ELEVEN

WHICH of them had he startled the most, Stephanie…or himself?

And yet, as soon as David had spoken the words, he knew they made sense.

He'd avoided the truth for years, but here it was, staring him in the face. It was time he got himself a wife.

Mary and Jack Russell were right. A man in his position needed one, and she couldn't be just any wife. He needed a woman who'd understand the social, as well as the business, aspects of his lifestyle. She'd have to entertain clients, give dinner parties and feel at ease with the people he dealt with, despite their titles and importance on the Washington scene. Until now, he'd relied upon whatever woman was in his life at the moment to play hostess, but that wasn't the same as having a wife to oversee the planning—or to sit beside you on the sofa when the evening ended, kick off her shoes and share a quiet moment.

Not that he'd expect that of Stephanie. It had never really been like that with Krissie and he wasn't foolish enough to think it would be any different this time around, but at least this arrangement would be an honest one, with all the expectations out in the open.

He'd learned from his mistakes. The first time he'd married, he'd been young and foolish; he'd thought you chose a woman with your heart. He knew better now. Choosing a wife was like choosing a car. He always bought Porsches, as much for their beauty and performance as for their workmanship. An intelligent man could apply the same standards to his choice of a mate. You wanted a good-looking model with superior ability, one that wouldn't disappoint in tough situations.

Stephanie filled the bill. She was beautiful; she was bright, she'd understand what would be expected of her, and she had no more illusions about marriage than he did.

There it was. He needed a wife. She needed a provider. It was an arrangement that would work. All he had to do was convince Stephanie, who was staring at him as if he'd just suggested they spend the weekend on Mars.

"Did you say…did you ask me to marry you, David?"

"Yes," he said calmly, "I did."

"Marry?" she said, looking bewildered. Well, he couldn't blame her for that. "You, and me?"

"That's right, Scarlett. You, and me."

"This is a joke, right?" Stephanie started to smile, then read the answer in his eyes. "My God! You're serious!"

"I am, indeed."

"Why?" She hesitated, then touched the tip of her tongue to the center of her bottom lip. "You aren't saying—you don't mean... You haven't—"

"Fallen in love with you?" He smiled and shook his head, as if she'd made a sad attempt at humor. "Of course not."

"Well, that's a relief," Stephanie said, giving the same little smile in return, because it was better than wondering why her pulse was racing.

"Love doesn't enter into this." He folded his arms; his expression grew serious. "That's what makes my proposal so reasonable."

"Reasonable?" She shook her head. "To you, maybe. Why on earth would we want to marry? I don't understand."

There was a trill of laughter from the house. David frowned and looked over his shoulder. The party had spilled onto the terrace.

"Let's walk," he said brusquely, and took her elbow. She didn't move, and he jerked her forward. She hurried to match his pace as he drew her deeper into the garden. "All right," he said when they'd left the house far behind, "let me put this so you *can* understand."

"I wish you would."

"A couple of months ago, I arranged for a corporate merger."

She gave a brittle laugh. "You see us as the new Procter and Gamble?"

"Each of the companies had different strengths," he said, deciding her nervous attempt at humor didn't merit a response. "One had—I suppose you'd call it power. The other had, well, a certain flair for doing things."

"Let me guess," Stephanie said. "You've got the power. And I've got—what did you call it? Flair?"

A breeze ruffled the rosebushes behind them and blew a strand of hair across her cheek. David reached out and tucked it behind her ear.

"For lack of a better word, yes."

"David, I still have no idea what you're talking about."

"I'm trying to explain the benefits of marriage. Let me try by telling you what I stand to gain." He cleared his throat. "Being a bachelor in this town isn't easy."

Stephanie smiled. "Do that many Mimi Sheratons pop out of the woodwork?"

"I know it must seem amusing, but trust me, Scarlett, it's not. And then there are the Annie Coopers, and the Mary Russells—Jack's wife— ladies who wake up in the morning and ask themselves, what man can I marry off today?'' He sighed. ''It gets to you, after a while.''

''I'm sure it does,'' Stephanie said politely.

David scowled. ''Look, I know I'm not making a good job of this...''

''No,'' she said, even more politely, ''you're doing fine. You want a wife, to keep you safe from matchmakers and predatory females. Or is there more?''

''This isn't funny, Scarlett. I'm serious.''

''I can see that. Go on. You said there was more.''

''Well, there are my professional responsibilities.''

''I'm already working as your secretary, David. What more could I possibly—''

''Okay. Okay, I'm making this sound like—like—''

''Like a merger. But then, that's exactly what you said it was.''

''Hell!'' David put his fists on his hips and glared at her. ''Why must you make this so difficult? I'm talking about the kind of life I live. There are parties. Dinners. All kinds of functions...''

''And you need a wife, to oversee them.''

''Yes,'' he said with a relieved smile. At last, she was getting it. ''That's right, I do.''

"So you said to yourself, 'Self, I need a wife. One who can plan a dinner party, make small talk, you know the routine.' And your Self said, 'Well, there's always Stephanie Willingham. She's done this kind of thing before.'"

"No," David said quickly, "it wasn't like that."

"Of course it was." Stephanie flashed a quick smile. "Think of the benefits, David. No on-the-job training needed. Right?"

"Dammit, Scarlett—"

"No. No, really, I understand. Truly, I do." Her voice quavered a little, which was dumb. Why would it upset her, that David would offer her the same arrangement she'd had before? It made absolute sense—for him. "But, what's that saying? Been there, done that. And I'd be a fool to do it again."

"I'm not suggesting a repeat of your first marriage. I'm not Willingham. Haven't you figured that out by now?"

"I hoped I had," she said, speaking carefully, not wanting to let him know how hurt she was. "But here you are, making me the same offer."

"The hell I am!"

"You are! There's no difference."

"Sure there is."

"Name one."

"For starters, I'll direct Jack to write a pre-nup, guaranteeing you a generous income for the rest of your life, no matter what happens to me."

"I don't need your money. It's for—"

"Your little brother. I understand that. I'm just pointing out that you wouldn't be left destitute, if I weren't around. And I won't dole money out to you, month by month. I'll deposit…" He paused and did some quick mental math. "I'll put five hundred thousand dollars into your checking account, Monday morning."

Stephanie stared at him. Half a million dollars? He was serious! But why?

"Why?" she said. "Why would you do all that, David? You're not a man who needs to—to buy a wife."

Why? he thought. It was a good question. Could he answer it, without looking too deeply inside himself?

"Because you and I can be up-front about what each of us expects from this marriage," he said.

"You want a relationship that's so—so cold-blooded?"

"I was married before. We were in love, or so I thought," he said bluntly. "It was a disaster."

"What happened?"

An image flashed through David's mind, of Krissie, in bed with her lover. It still hurt. The fact of the adultery, yes, and the divorce…but it was the betrayal that had devastated him.

He shrugged. "It turned out we each had different ideas about marriage."

"Lots of people are divorced, David. They don't end up trying to—to buy a spouse."

"Are you being deliberately dense? I'm not trying to buy you!"

"Really?" Stephanie folded her arms. "Well, that's how it sounds to me."

"Then you're not paying attention or you'd understand that I'm outlining a marriage in which each of us contributes something of value."

"What I understand," Stephanie said, "is that I won't make the same mistake twice." She stepped back, her head at a proud angle. "Thank you for your offer, David, but I'm not interested."

"Scarlett, you're not thinking. You're—"

"Damn you!" She flew at him, moving so fast that he didn't have time to duck, and pounded her fists against his shoulders. "A marriage *needs* feelings! *I* need feelings. I need—"

"I know what you need," David said, and pulled her into his arms.

His mouth was warm, his arms strong. She struggled against him for the time it took her heart to take one suddenly erratic beat and then she admitted the truth to herself, that she was struggling not against David but against what she felt, and she wound her arms around his neck and kissed him back with all the hunger inside her.

"Marry me," he whispered.

She hesitated, and he kissed her again.

"Scarlett. Just take a deep breath and say yes."

Stephanie looked at him. Then she took the breath he'd suggested.

"Yes."

They left the Sheraton house without making their goodbyes, and drove to Georgetown.

David's house was dark, and silent. The sound of the door, shutting behind them, echoed against the night.

Stephanie could hear the thud-thud of her own heart. She was trembling. She'd accused David of being crazy, but she was the crazy one. What had she agreed to? She, of all people. Why would she agree to this marriage? To become this stranger's wife? She couldn't go through with the marriage, or with what would come next. It was one thing to feel the stir of desire in David's embrace but to act upon it, to think, even for a moment, she'd feel what a woman was supposed to feel when a man touched her...

"David," she said urgently, "I think—"

"Don't think," he said, and took her in his arms.

He kissed her over and over, each kiss deeper, hungrier, than the last until she was clinging to his shoulders.

''Scarlett,'' he whispered, and swung her into his arms.

Stephanie looped her hands behind David's head. A pale ribbon of creamy light streamed in through the window. In its faint illumination, she could see the need etched into his face.

''I've never wanted a woman as I want you, Scarlett,'' he said softly.

''David.'' She swallowed audibly. ''I can't… I'm not…I don't much like sex. You have the right to know that. I'll disappoint—''

His kiss silenced her. ''Never,'' he whispered, and carried her up the stairs.

She had not been in his bedroom until this night.

It was austere, what little she could see of it in the shadowed dark, what little she could concentrate on, other than the hot pounding of her own blood.

David put her down, slowly, beside the bed.

''There's nothing to be afraid of, Scarlett.'' He cupped her face in his hands, bent his head and brushed his mouth gently over hers.

''I'm not afraid,'' she said, ''I know you won't hurt me.''

It wasn't true. He *would* hurt her. Not physically. She knew that. He was nothing like Avery, who had taken pleasure from the pain of others. But she was vulnerable to David in other ways, ones that could result in a far deeper pain, because she felt—she felt—

"David." She caught his hands as he reached for her. "This is a mistake. We shouldn't marry."

"We can be happy," he said gruffly. "Did you ever think of that?"

She wanted to. Oh, she wanted to. He saw it in her eyes, the hope, the desire…

"Scarlett?" he said, and she went into his arms.

He undressed her slowly, baring her skin to his mouth and hands inch by silken inch. She was even more beautiful than he'd imagined, her breasts high and rounded, her waist slender, her hips almost as narrow as a boy's. She felt like silk, tasted like vanilla, smelled like some exotic flower. By the time she lay naked in his arms, he was breathing hard and fast.

"Scarlett." He reached out, traced the tip of his finger down her throat, over the swell of her breast, down, down, down until it rested just above the soft curls that guarded her feminine self. "You are so beautiful, Scarlett. So perfect…" His hand moved, dipped between her thighs, and she gasped and caught hold of his wrist.

"David." Her voice was thready. "I don't... Could we pull up the blankets?"

"Are you cold, love? I'll warm you."

Love. He had called her "love."

"No." She shook her head, wondering why there should be a sudden dampness on her cheeks. "I'm not cold, David. I'm—it's the way you're looking at me. I feel—embarrassed."

He smiled. "That's because you're undressed and I'm not. But we can fix that."

He rose to his feet, his eyes never leaving hers, and stripped off his clothing. The body he revealed was beautiful and powerful. Even the frightening part, that most masculine part, was beautiful. He lay down beside her again, his hair loose, floating like a dark curtain around their faces as he took her in his arms.

"Better?" he whispered.

She nodded. His skin was hot, his body hard. She could feel his arousal against her belly and she waited for the excitement to ebb and the panic to start, but it didn't. Instead, she felt a throbbing heat begin to spread between her thighs.

"David," she said unsteadily. "You're so beautiful."

He laughed softly. "How can a man be beautiful, sweetheart?" Her breath caught as he bent and tongued her nipple. "This is beautiful," he whispered. His head dipped lower; he kissed her belly. "And this." He moved again, and she moaned as she felt the heat of his breath between her thighs. "And this," he said, his voice gruff. "Open for me, Scarlett," he said.

And she did.

She shattered at the first kiss, arching against his mouth. Surely she'd have flown into the sky, into the night, if his hands hadn't been curved around her hips, holding her against him. Just as she was falling back to earth, he rose above her and kissed her mouth. She tasted the miracle of their shared passion on his tongue.

"David," she said in a whisper so filled with awe and joy that it was almost his undoing. "David, please..."

"Yes," he said, and he entered her, trying to do it gently, slowly, wanting to pleasure her and not hurt her, wanting to give her everything, not just his body and his seed but his heart.

She cried out in wonder, moved against him, and he let go of everything, the taut control and the anger that had defined his life for so long. He sank into Stephanie's welcoming heat and let himself, at long last, find happiness.

She said she could cook.

"Red beans and rice," she said, "hush puppies, fried catfish...'' She looked over her shoulder at him and smiled. ''Except I don't see any of those things in these cabinets, David.''

David smiled back. It was near dawn. They were in his kitchen, Stephanie was at the stove and he was straddling a chair, his chin resting on his folded arms. Hunger had driven them from the bed. Nothing else could have. He'd made love to her all night, and he still wanted her so badly he ached. But the ache was worthwhile, if it meant watching his future wife search the shelves. She was wearing the white shirt he'd discarded when they'd arrived home last night. Just the shirt. Nothing more.

''It doesn't cover very much, David,'' she'd said, blushing as he buttoned her into it.

''It covers everything,'' he'd said, lying through his teeth, because hell, he was not a saint, he was a man. Seeing the sweet curve of her breasts, the faint darkness at the juncture of her thighs; enjoying the length of her legs and the occasional glimpse of her backside as she reached for something on the top shelf, was more than he could possibly pass up.

By God, he was lucky! It amazed him, to have found this woman. She was everything a man could hope for. Beautiful. Bright. Capable. And sexy enough to steal his breath away, even though she didn't know it.

"I don't much like sex," she'd said, but she'd been incredible in bed. Warm. Eager. Giving. Everything he had done to her, for her, she had wanted to do in return. She'd gone from restraint to recklessness, and it had driven him half out of his head. Even thinking about it made things happen to his anatomy.

That bastard, Willingham. He'd never deserved Stephanie. Whatever he'd done to her… No. He couldn't think about it. It was just a good thing the man was dead because if he wasn't—if he wasn't…

"Bacon and eggs?"

David blinked. Stephanie was looking at him inquiringly. She had a skillet in one hand and a package of bacon in the other, and he knew she wanted him to tell her what he wanted for breakfast, but God, all he really wanted to tell her was that he loved her, that he'd always loved her, that fate or kismet or whatever you wanted to call it had brought them together at that wedding…

"David?"

He took a deep breath. "Fine," he said calmly. "Sounds great. I'll do the toast and coffee."

And work on regaining his equilibrium, along with his sanity. This wasn't love, it was lust.

"Let me just get down this bowl," Stephanie said, and reached high to the top shelf.

David kicked back his chair. "To hell with breakfast," he said.

The skillet, and the bacon, fell from her hands. "Yes," she said, and then she was in his arms again, where he knew she had always belonged.

He broke the news to Jack over lunch on Monday.

"You're nuts," Jack said flatly.

"Maybe," David said, smiling.

Jack lifted his martini. "Wonderful. I tell the groom he's crazy and the groom says, 'Maybe.'"

"I'm also happy."

"Even better. My ol' granpappy used to say—he used to say..." Jack gulped half his martini. "Who knows what the old so-and-so used to say? What *I* say is that you're loco. The lady gets a bank account. What do you get?"

"A wife. Ask Mary. She'll tell you it's an equitable trade."

"Did you check her out? Did you check out the sick brother?"

"No," David said tightly. "I told you, this all happened very suddenly."

"Think about the lady's past, David. She married for money once before. Now, she's doing it again. For all you know, the *brother* could be a gambling habit. He could be drugs."

"She's not on drugs, Jack. And she's not a gambler."

"Well, then, he could be a lover with expensive tastes."

"Watch what you say," David said coldly. "This time next week, Stephanie will be my wife."

Jack refused to back down. "Look, phone Dan Nolan. Let him do a little research. I'm surprised you haven't already done it."

David's eyes narrowed. Stephanie, supporting a lover? He'd never even thought...

He rose quickly, slapped a few bills on the table. "I've got a meeting," he said when Jack started to protest, "and I'm running late."

"What kind of groom says 'maybe' when you tell him he's crazy?" Jack Russell demanded of his wife, late that night.

Mary patted her husband's hand. "The kind who's not ready to admit he's in love."

Jack snorted. "Don't be ridiculous. He's infatuated."

"He's in love," Mary said. "All we can do now is hope he doesn't get hurt."

That evening, before she left the office, Stephanie phoned Rest Haven. Paul's nurse took the call. Paul didn't want to speak to her. He was depressed. Stephanie almost laughed. Paul was always depressed, but she understood. This was worse than usual. It was not a good sign.

"Call me, if anything happens," she said. Then she hung up the phone and stared blindly at the wall.

Paul had been doing so well. Was he going to have a relapse? It didn't matter. She still had to tell David more about him. Soon, David would be her husband. He'd be paying for Paul's care. And she wanted no secrets between her and the man she—the man she...

"Ready?"

She looked up. David was standing in the doorway. His smile had an edge that unnerved her.

"David? What is it? Is something wrong?"

David hesitated. Yes, he wanted to say, something *was* wrong. He'd spent the afternoon pacing his office and finally, half an hour ago, he'd put in a call to Dan Nolan, asked him to check on Stephanie and find out what he could about her brother. If she had a brother. If Jack hadn't put his finger on the truth...

Enough!

"No," he said. "It's just been a long day. Let's go home."

An uneasy silence lay between them through dinner and on into the evening. Finally, David put aside the papers he'd been trying to read and looked at Stephanie.

"Scarlett?"

She looked up from her book. There was a strained look on her face.

"Yes?"

David thought of the call he'd made to Dan Nolan. He regretted it, now. He had questions, yes, but he should have asked them of Stephanie. This was supposed to be an honest relationship.

"What, David?"

Ask her, he told himself. Tell her you need to know more about her brother, that you want to meet him…

"Nothing," he said after a minute. "Just…" He took her hand. "It's late," he said. "Let's go up."

He undressed her slowly in the darkness of the bedroom, loving the sounds she made as he touched her, the scent of desire that rose from her skin. His concerns fell away from him as they went into each other's arms. This was right. *She* was right. This could work…

The phone rang.

"David? The telephone…"

"Let it ring," he said, but he sighed, kissed her gently, turned on the bedside lamp and lifted the receiver.

Stephanie sat up against the pillows, the blanket to her chin. David was turned away from her, the blanket at his waist. His naked shoulders and back were pale gold in the faint gleam of the light. The call couldn't be for her, yet she knew it was. Paul, she thought, it's Paul.

David turned and looked at her. He held out the telephone.

"It's a man," he said. His face was expressionless. "He won't give his name. He wants to talk to you."

Stephanie took the phone. "Hello?"

It *was* Paul. His voice was calm, controlled. He said the nurse had given him Stephanie's new phone number.

"Where are you?" Stephanie said.

He told her. He'd slipped out of Rest Haven. He was in a motel.

Stephanie nodded. Rest Haven was a care facility, not a prison.

"I need you, Sis," Paul said.

She looked at David. There was still no expression on his face.

"I'll come in the morning," she said. "Meanwhile, you should—"

"I need you now."

She looked at David again. Then she reached for the pad and pencil on the nightstand.

"Tell me where you are," she said, and wrote it down. She licked her dry lips. "I'll come." The phone went dead, and she handed it to David, who hung it up.

"David? I—I have to go to my brother."

David's eyes were as flat and dull as the sea before a storm. "At this hour?"

"Yes."

"Why? What's the problem?"

"He's ill. Look, I know you have questions, but I can't explain now." She started to rise, remembered she was naked under the blanket, and knew she couldn't endure the feel of his cool gaze on her skin. "Could you—would you turn around, please?"

David's jaw clenched. "Such modesty, Scarlett," he said with a hard smile, but he turned his back and she rose quickly and began pulling on her clothes.

She heard a noise behind her. David had flung back the blanket. He was dressing.

"What are you doing?"

"What does it look like I'm doing?" He yanked a sweatshirt from a drawer and tugged it over his head. "I'm getting dressed."

"No, David. It isn't necessary."

He looked at her. "I'm not going to let you go out, alone, in the middle of the night."

"I'll be fine. I'll call a cab."

"I can drive you wherever it is you're going."

"No!" She thought of Paul, as he would be now, knowing how much worse things could get if he were to be upset. "No, David, really. You don't have to."

"I know that. I *want* to go with you."

"But *I* don't want you with me!" The words fell between them like stones. Stephanie caught her breath. "David. I didn't mean that the way it sounded."

"You'll find the number of a cab company programmed into the phone downstairs," he said coldly. Then he walked into the bathroom, and shut the door.

The motel looked like a set from a cheap movie.

Paul was in the last room. He lay in bed, under the covers, with his arm over his eyes, and he was as bad as she'd ever seen him. His clothing lay discarded on the floor.

"Paul?" she said softly.

He didn't respond. She sighed, shut the door behind her, and went to him. She knew what to do. She'd sit beside him, cradle him in her arms, tell him how much she loved him and hope against hope that her words would sink in...and that, when she explained, David would understand. She thought of how he'd looked at her and a shudder racked her body.

She would not lose David. She could not lose him, and it hadn't a damn thing to do with needing money, or what he'd miraculously made her feel in bed.

It was time to admit the truth. She was in love with David, and she could only hope that he might love her, too, someday.

David paced up and down his living room.

What in hell did Stephanie think she was doing? Going off in the middle of the night to see her sick brother? Telling him, hell, *shrieking* at him, that she didn't want him to go with her?

If it was a brother, he thought grimly.

For all he knew, Jack was right. There was no brother. There was a man, yeah, but not one related to her. It would explain so much. So much. The reason she needed money, that she'd tolerated Willingham's abuse...

That she was so good, so incredibly good, in bed.

David stopped pacing. He felt cold, as if the marrow of his bones were turning to ice. Women lied. Krissie had taught him that. They were faithless. Krissie had taught him that, too.

But Krissie, at least, hadn't married a man for money.

Why hadn't he asked Nolan to check on Stephanie before this? He needed something to go on...

And then he remembered. She had scrawled something on the notepad.

He ran up the stairs, snatched up the pad. The impression left by the pencil was deep and clear. David read it, and the coldness seeped away. Rage, white-hot and glowing, replaced it.

"Damn you, Stephanie," he whispered.

And then he was out of the house, in his Porsche, roaring toward the Elmsview Motel.

"Paul," Stephanie said. "Paul, please, can you hear me?"

She shifted closer to her brother, lifted his head and cradled it against her shoulder. "Please, Paul. Talk to me."

Paul made a strangled sound. He rolled over, clutched her tightly and buried his face in her breast.

"Oh, Paul," she said softly. She bent her head, kissed his hair. "Darling, I love you. You know I do. No matter what happens, I'll always be here for you. I love you, Paul. I love..."

The door slammed against the wall, and the stink of the highway suddenly filled the room. Stephanie turned quickly and saw David standing in the doorway.

"David? David, what are you doing here?"

His gaze swept over the room, taking in the discarded clothing, the rumpled bed, the man in her arms. Something hot and dark twisted inside him.

"Such a trite question, Scarlett. At least I don't have to ask it of you. We both know what *you're* doing here."

"No. Whatever you're thinking..."

David's hands knotted into fists. The man, the scurvy bastard, had barely moved. The urge to stride across the room, drag Stephanie from the bed by the scruff of her lying neck, beat the crap out of her lover, roared through him like a tidal wave. But, if he did, he'd never stop. He'd beat her lover until he was a bloody pulp, and then he'd turn on Stephanie and he'd—he'd...

God, oh, God, what did you do when the woman you loved tore out your heart?

He blinked hard, forcing the red haze to clear from his eyes.

"Not to worry, Scarlett." From somewhere, he dredged up a smile. "We were both playing games. You just got careless before I did, that's all."

Her face, her lovely face, became even paler than it already was.

"What games?"

He laughed. "You didn't really think I was going to marry you, did you? Hey, a man will do a
lot of things to get a woman into his bed, but
marry her? Not me, baby. I'm not a fool like
Willingham."

She recoiled, as if she'd been struck. He turned
on his heel, victorious, and strode from the sleazy
little room, telling himself he'd forever remember
this moment.

But it wasn't true. He got into his car, shut the
door and pounded his fists against the steering
wheel while the tears coursed down his face,
knowing that what he'd always remember was the
agony of Stephanie's betrayal.

It would be with him for the rest of his life.

CHAPTER TWELVE

THERE was no place on earth as beautiful as Wyoming in June. David had always thought so, even when he was a kid growing up in a clapboard shack in a cowtown slum.

He'd come a long way since then, a hell of a long way. The thought brought a smile to his face for the first time in days, but then, he'd almost always found something to make him smile, when he was up here, on the ridge that overlooked the Bar C Ranch.

Night was coming. Purple shadows were already stretching their long fingers over the mountains. A red-tailed hawk, still seeking his dinner, drifted on silent wings across the canyon.

David's horse snorted and danced sideways with impatience. He reached forward and patted the velvet-soft neck.

"Easy, boy," he said softly.

The horse had had enough of sunsets. And so had he. It was getting him nowhere, sitting on this damned bluff every evening, watching the mountains and the hawk...and imagining.

He frowned, tugged at the reins, and turned for the trail that led down to the valley, and home.

''Stupid,'' he muttered.

Stupid was the word. What else could you call a man who'd been lucky enough to avoid disaster by the thinnest margin, who'd come within a whisper of tying himself to a woman who lied and cheated as easily as some people breathed? What was such a man, if not stupid, when he ended up thinking about her, remembering each detail of her face, instead of being forever grateful he'd gotten away with his skin intact?

There was no reason to think about Stephanie anymore. She was out of his life, and he was thankful for it.

''Thank heavens you came to your senses,'' Jack had said when David had brusquely informed him that the wedding was off, and he hadn't argued. Jack was right.

Then, why couldn't he get her out of his head?

It was almost dark now. His horse knew the trail well but still, the animal's ears were pricked forward and he made his way with care. That was fine. David was in no rush to get back to the house. His housekeeper would have supper waiting, he'd go through the charade of telling her how fine the meal was, move the stuff around on his plate a little so it looked as if he'd done more than pick at it, and then he'd go sit in the parlor, build a fire to ward off the chill that still settled on the mountains, even in June. He'd read, or work on some legal stuff he'd brought with him…pretend to read, or work, to be accurate. And then he'd look at the clock, tell himself it was time for bed, and go upstairs, alone, to toss and turn in the big canopied bed where he'd once imagined himself lying with Stephanie in his arms.

David frowned. Where in hell had that bit of nonsense come from? He'd never even thought of bringing her here. She wasn't the outdoors type—was she? He really didn't know. And, dammit, he really didn't care.

Why didn't he stop thinking about her?

His horse whinnied and David realized they'd come out of the trees. Dusk had settled over the valley. The house, nestled against the spectacular mountain backdrop, looked cozy and warm. It had the look and feel he'd always thought a home should have, even years ago, when he'd only been able to dream about living in a place like this.

He couldn't recall much about the house where he'd been born. His folks had been poor; they'd died when he was just a little kid and he'd gone to live in a foster home where the man he was ordered to address as "Dad" thought beatings and poverty were necessary for the good of the soul. That house he could remember with utmost clarity. The rooms had been uniformly gray, but neither the surroundings nor the people had been able to ruin the view.

The view had been David's salvation.

If you scrambled up the drainpipe to the flat roof, you could see past the streets and the clutter to the mountains. He'd spent a lot of time on that roof, looking at the mountains, telling himself that someday he'd live up there, in a place where you could almost reach up and touch the sky. It had seemed an impossible dream but he was living proof that dreams could, indeed, come true. Everything here was his. The valley, the house, the mountains—all of it.

Luck, hard work, a combination of things had secured him this existence. The football scholarship had come first, then an academic scholarship to Yale Law, and, at last, a career he loved. So he'd had a failed marriage along the way. Those things happened to lots of people. He'd been bitter, but he'd survived. And, until a couple of weeks ago, he'd figured he had everything a man could possibly want in life.

Now, he knew better.

What he needed was someone to share all this with. No. Not someone.

Stephanie.

David's jaw tightened. That was crazy. He didn't need her. Why would he?

It infuriated him, that he should even think of her. What a time she must have had, not to have collapsed with laughter when he'd asked her if she had any acting experience. Experience? She had enough to open her own drama school. She'd spent her years with Willingham at stage center. As for the short time she'd spent with him... damn, but she'd outdone any performance he'd ever watched on the Broadway stage.

It wasn't as if he'd really loved her. Oh, sure, he'd been infatuated. He'd even sat outside that fleabag motel, convinced he'd never get over her, but he had. It didn't hurt to think about her anymore. What thinking about her did was make him angry.

"Angry as hell," he said, and the horse danced nervously again.

No man liked to be played for a fool, and that was exactly what Stephanie had done to him.

He'd admitted that to Jack.

"She played me for a fool," he'd said over a three-bourbon lunch.

Jack had sighed and shaken his head; he'd looked down into his drink and over the heads of the diners at the next table, anywhere but at David, and he'd said, in a voice that could have rung with self-righteous satisfaction but didn't, "I tried to warn you, David."

Yes. Oh, yes. Jack had tried to warn him, but he'd been so sure. So convinced. So damn positive he'd found...

What?

What had he thought he'd found? An honest woman? Stephanie had never been that. A woman with simple tastes? No way. A woman who loved him? Absolutely not. Well, that was something, wasn't it? She hadn't ever claimed to love him. And a good thing, too, because he'd have called her on it. He'd have known she was handing him a load of crap because a woman who loved a man didn't lie, didn't cheat, didn't weep crocodile tears.

It was just that he couldn't forget. Her laugh. Her smile. The way she'd get that glint in her eye and stand up to him, no matter what...

The way she whispered his name when they made love, in a voice hushed with emotion. The way she returned his kisses. The way she curled into him when she slept, with her head on his shoulder and her arm across his chest, as if she never wanted to let him go...

"Dammit," he snarled.

Startled, the horse reared up on its hind legs. When its hooves touched the ground, David dug in his heels and leaned forward. He knew better than to hope he could leave his memories behind, but maybe, if he was lucky, he could ride and ride and ride, until he was just too tired to think anymore.

Riding helped.

So did working hard every day, from sunrise until sunset. He knew his men were asking each other questions behind his back. Even his foreman, who knew him as well as anybody and knew, too, that he'd always worked as hard as any of the hands, started looking at him strangely.

Nobody would ask him any questions, though, partly because he was the boss, mostly because you just didn't do that. In the West, a man's thoughts were his own. And that was just as well, David told himself as he sweated over what had to be his millionth fence posthole of the afternoon, because anybody getting a look at what he was thinking would have run for cover.

Why had he ever gone to the Cooper wedding? Why had he sat at table seven? Why had he let Jack talk him into going to Georgia?

Because he was an idiot, that was why. David grunted and jammed the digger into the soil. Because he was an unmitigated, unrepentant ass, that was why.

"David?"

He looked up. His foreman was standing in front of him, his hands on his hips.

"What?" he snapped.

"You have a phone call." The foreman looked down at the ground, then up at David. "You're also about to dig that next hole right through your foot."

David looked at the posthole digger, then at his boot. He cursed, tossed the digger aside and wiped the sweat out of his eyes.

"I'm not in such a great mood lately," he said.

His foreman raised his eyebrows. "Do tell."

The two men looked at each other.

"I guess it shows."

"Nah."

His foreman grinned. David smiled back.

"Thanks for the message," he said.

The foreman nodded. "Sure." He watched his boss stride toward the house. Then he sighed, shrugged his shoulders, and headed back to the barns.

The house was cool and quiet. David nodded to his housekeeper and signaled that he'd take the call in the library. He shut the door after him, took the phone from the desk, and put it to his ear.

"This had better be good, Jack," he said.

He heard his partner laugh.

"That's quite a greeting, David. How could you be so sure it's me?"

"No one else would be foolhardy enough to call me here." David cocked a hip against the edge of his desk. "What do you want, Jack? I told you, when I left, that I was going to take a few weeks off."

"I know, but..." Jack cleared his throat. "I thought you might want to hear this."

"Hear what? The only open file I've got is that Palmer thing, and I explained—"

"It's not about the office, David." Jack cleared his throat again. "It's about the Willingham woman."

David's heart dropped. "What about her? Has something happened to her? Is she—"

"No, no, it's not about her. Not exactly. It's...the report came in."

"What report?"

"The one from Dan Nolan. You asked him to do a check on her, remember?"

David closed his eyes. A sharp pain lanced just behind his eyes. "Yeah," he said, rubbing the bridge of his nose. "I remember. Listen, do me a favor, Jack. Burn it."

"Well, I was going to, David. But then Dan phoned, and he said some things..."

"What things?"

"Look, I think you might be interested in what he found out."

"Yeah, well, I'm not. Just take the report and—"

"I sent it out this morning, David. By courier."

David sighed. ''No problem. I'll chuck it out when it arrives.''

But he didn't.

The report arrived early the next morning. David took it into the library, along with a mug of black coffee. He sat down at his desk, tilted back his chair, put his feet up and studied the envelope as it lay on his desk. Then he sat up straight, drank the coffee, and squared the edge of the envelope with the edge of the desk. It was a standard number nine tan manila envelope, no different than a thousand other envelopes...

He dreaded opening it.

''Dammit, Chambers, stop being a jerk.''

He moved quickly, grabbing the envelope and ripping it open. A slim white folder was inside. Dan's letter was attached but he ignored it, looked at the folder and took a deep breath.

There it was, waiting for him. The story of Stephanie's life. Not as many pages as he'd have figured, but quantity wasn't everything, quality was.

His smile was bittersweet.

Read it, he told himself, and put an end to thinking about her. He took another deep breath.

'''And the truth shall set you free,''' he murmured.

He opened the folder.

An hour later, he sat with the pages of the report scattered on the desktop.

"Oh, Scarlett," he whispered. "Scarlett, my love."

By midday, he was seated in the cockpit of a chartered plane, headed for Willingham Corners, Georgia. The pilot, a man he'd known most of his adult life, chattered on and on about the world and the weather, but all David could think about was Stephanie, and how much he loved her...

And how badly he had failed her.

Stephanie sat shelling peas on the tiny porch of the house she'd grown up in.

It was a warm, lazy afternoon. Fat honeybees buzzed among the roses; an oriole trilled from the lowest branch of a magnolia. It was a perfect June day—or it would have been, if she weren't so angry.

"Idiot," she muttered, snapping open a pod and slipping the peas into the bowl in her lap.

She wasn't just angry. She was furious, and at herself. She had been, for weeks.

She blew a strand of hair out of her eyes and picked up another pea pod.

Oh, she'd wasted some time on stupidity, crying over losing David, but that hadn't lasted long. Why would it? You couldn't lose what you'd never had, and she had never "had" David. Why would she have wanted to have him? What had she seen in him, anyway? He was a liar, a cheat, and a scoundrel, just like all the rest of them.

"Avery incarnate," she mumbled, and slammed the peas into the bowl.

To think she'd imagined herself in love with such a rat. To think she'd wanted to marry him. To think she'd slept with him...

Except, she hadn't slept with him. She'd made love with him, and yes, there was a difference. A wonderful difference. Otherwise she'd never have felt the things she'd felt, never have died and been reborn in his arms.

"Nonsense," she said briskly.

And it *was* nonsense. She'd been vulnerable, that was all. David had come along when she was having a difficult time. He'd shown her what she'd thought was kindness, but it had turned out to be nothing but a scheme to get her into his bed.

It was hard to believe any man would go to such lengths just to seduce a woman, especially a man like David. Stephanie's throat constricted. She'd been so sure it was all real. The kindness. The decency. The concern.

The love. Oh, David's love. His kisses and caresses. His whispered promises. His tenderness.

Stephanie gave herself a little shake.

"Stop it," she said sternly.

The lies, for that was what they'd been, were all behind her. David was the past. The future...well, she wasn't sure just what the future was, but it was shaping up. She smiled and brushed her hand over her eyes. Things were definitely going to get better. Paul, for one. He *was* better. New medications had made a big improvement. And a day after she'd pleaded with Rest Haven's management board, explained how desperate she was, they'd come up with an incredible proposal. They'd halve the cost of Paul's care, if she'd agree to replace the administrative assistant to the manager, when she retired in two weeks.

So now, here she was, spending a quiet time at the old family homestead before beginning her new job. Yes, life was good. It was fine. It was...

Oh, God, it was a mess, because David, damn him, had broken her heart. Who was she kidding? She hated him. Despised him. But that didn't keep her from dreaming about him, from longing for the comfort of his arms—

"Scarlett?"

The bowl tumbled from her lap and Stephanie shot to her feet. She spun around, her hand to her breast, knowing, *knowing,* that she had to be imagining the sound of David's voice...

But she wasn't.

"David," she whispered, and her heart kicked against her ribs.

He stood no more than twenty feet away, not moving, not talking, just looking at her. What was he doing here? How had he found her?

What did he want?

"You," he said, and she knew she must have spoken the last question aloud.

Her heart did another little tumble. Don't, she told herself. Oh, Steffie, don't. He's lying. He must be lying. And even if he isn't, you know what he believes. What he thinks...

"I love you, Scarlett."

Her mouth began to tremble. "No," she said, and shook her head. Her hands were trembling, too, and she stuck them deep into the pockets of her old jeans. "Please, don't say that."

"I don't deserve another chance," he said as he started slowly toward her. "I know that. I failed you, sweetheart. When you needed me the most, I wasn't there."

"No." Stephanie shook her head again. "Don't, David. I can't—I can't bear it."

"I didn't trust you. I knew it, and I told myself that was fine, that a man had to be a fool to trust a woman." He stopped at the foot of the porch steps and looked into her eyes. They were shining with tears and he resisted the desire to reach out, pull her down into his arms and kiss the tears away. "I love you," he said again. "I want you to be my wife."

Stephanie took a step back. "This isn't fair," she whispered. "To say these things and—and not mean them…"

He smiled. "I'm a lawyer, Scarlett. Would a lawyer tell a lie?"

"Isn't that what they do?" she said, her head lifting with defiance.

David sighed. "Well, yeah. Sometimes, I guess, but only by omission."

"*You* lied. And not by omission. You know you did."

He climbed the steps slowly, watching as she backed away from him, drinking in her beauty and the sweetness of her face, his heart suddenly blazing with hope because he knew, he *knew,* that she loved him just as much as he loved her.

"You're right," he said softly. Her shoulders hit the wall of the little clapboard house that looked strangely like the one he'd grown up in, and he smiled again, knowing she couldn't get away from him now, that he'd never let her get away from him again. "I did lie," he said, reaching out to touch her hair. "That's what I've come here to tell you."

"Don't—don't do that," she said, trying to pull away from him. He wouldn't let her. He just came closer, until she had to tilt her head to look up into his eyes, those wonderfully blue eyes.

''What do you mean, that's why you've come here?''

He stroked his hand over her hair, along her cheek. He cupped her shoulders with his palms and drew her unyielding body toward his.

''I came to tell you that I lied about everything, Scarlett.'' He put his hands into her hair and lifted her face to him. ''About not meaning it, when I proposed marriage.''

''It doesn't matter,'' she said stiffly. ''I wouldn't have—I never wanted to—please, David. Don't do that.''

He did it, anyway; he bent his head and brushed his mouth gently over hers. Stephanie held still. She didn't breathe. She wouldn't let him know what was happening to her, what his touch was doing to her...

A sob burst from her throat.

''Damn you,'' she whispered. ''You broke my heart, David. Wasn't that enough? Have you come here to do it again?''

''I came here to tell you that I love you,'' he said, ''that I've always loved you...and to beg your forgiveness.''

Stephanie looked up at him, her eyes wide.

''I love you, Scarlett. That's why I came up with that whole crazy scheme about why we should marry. I was too afraid to tell you the truth.''

"Afraid? Of what?"

"Of getting hurt. Of you saying you didn't love me."

"Oh, David." Stephanie smiled through her tears. "I love you with all my heart. But—but that night—the things you said…"

David kissed her. "Lies," he whispered, brushing the tears from her cheeks with his thumbs. "I saw you with another man and I went crazy with jealousy."

"It was Paul. My brother."

"I know that now."

"He's been sick for years, David, ever since he hit his head, a long time ago. I know I should have taken you to meet him. I wanted to, but Paul had—"

David kissed her again, holding her closely in his arms, so that she could feel the accelerated beat of his heart.

"You don't have to explain. I know everything, Scarlett, including what a fool I was, and if you let me, I'll spend the rest of my life proving how much I adore you. Will you marry me?"

Stephanie wrapped her arms around David's neck. "Yes," she said, her eyes shining, and David lifted her into his arms and carried her away from Willingham Corners forever.

*   *   *

They were married on the ranch, in Wyoming, on a gloriously warm and bright Sunday afternoon, two months later.

It would have been sooner, but it had taken time for David to arrange for Paul's admittance to a San Francisco clinic where remarkable progress was being made with injuries such as his.

"Anything you want to bet," David said softly to his bride on the morning of their wedding, "Paul will be well enough to celebrate our first anniversary with us here, on the Bar C."

Stephanie smiled, leaned up and kissed his cheek. She had no doubt it would happen, just the way David said. David always told the truth, and she trusted him with all her heart.

The wedding was small but perfect. All the guests said so, even Mary Russell, when she could stop weeping long enough to talk.

"You're being silly," Jack whispered to his wife, but he was smiling when he said it, and thinking what a lucky man he was to have her.

Annie couldn't come, but Stephanie promised to send pictures.

"You'll be a beautiful bride," Annie had promised, and everyone agreed that she was.

She wore a long, full gown of white silk with tiny silver flowers trimming the bodice, and carried a bouquet of baby's breath and tiny white and purple orchids. David wore a Western-cut tuxedo and black leather boots, and all the women sighed and said there'd never been a more handsome groom.

And when the day ended, and all the guests had left, he lifted Stephanie before him onto the saddle of his horse, just as she was, in all her bridal finery, and they rode up into the mountains, to watch the sun go down.

David turned her face up to his. "I love you, Scarlett."

Stephanie smiled radiantly. "I love you, too, my beloved husband," she murmured.

David kissed his bride. At long last, he was truly home.